Leave Your Money
on the Dresser

gibson grand

Flying Monkey Press
ISBN-13: 978-0615963914
ISBN-10: 0615963919

CONTENTS

Acknowledgements i

Celebration 1

Billy's Topless 7

Paris for Avenue C 9

The International Bar 10

The Beginning of History 12

Junkie Like Me 16

This City is a Drunken Mother 21

Sweet Bird of Youth (or I'm sorry, Tennessee) 22

Jambalaya and Negligee 23

Swan Lake 27

Return to Long Sleeves 29

Parlour Tricks 34

Painted Toes 35

Fireflies 37

Oklahoma Rose 42

Love Letter for Katelan 47

Drowning by the Fire 49

Nor'Easter 50

Second Story Window 51

Snow Angels 55

Jellyfish 59

There is a Motel Room in my Head 69

Unspoken (for Siren) 71

Treehouse 72

Ginny's Big Night 74

The Wig 78

The Lovers 83

What We Learn from Monarchs 84

Saint Hank 85

Contemplation 87

Trees of Heaven	95
Dream Catcher	97
The War of Bats and Porcupine	98
The Audacity of Love	99
Sparrow's Concern	100
Whisky Always Tastes Better on T.V.	102
Leave Your Money on the Dresser	104
The Wait	105
Glitter Hands	106
I Don't Want to Hold Your Hand	107
Poem for a Raleigh Prostitute	109
I Found Love at the Ooh La La	110
Nobody Fucks in Cars Anymore	118
What Fingers Are For	119
Everyday Casanova	120
Window Water Zombie Fucking	121
Accidental Betsy	123
Angel's Share	126
The Night Hotel	127
Words Are Too Frail (or Fuck Me Until I Don't Feel Sad Anymore)	128
Casual Encounter	129
Let Me Find Poetry	134
I Can Only Offer You My Flask	135

ACKNOWLEDGMENTS

These stories would not be possible without the ones who never made it—the men and women who fell through the cracks and to whom I am eternally grateful for gracing me with their presence.

I would not be possible without the unwavering support and guidance of the friends, both new and old, who have always encouraged me to just keep writing, including: Tom Vaught, the Reverend Timmy James, Guy New York, Paul Fox, Dave Horowitz, Jade Bos, Katie West, and Siren O'Brien. Thank you all. Your friendship speaks more volumes than I could ever write.

Special thanks to Jack Scoresby for the cover photography (featuring Aemilia McMorbid).

The stories, *Junkie Like Me*, *Return to Long Sleeves*, and *Swan Lake* were first published in the journal Transgressive Culture, © 2011 Gylphi Ltd.

"We are all in the gutter,
but some of us are looking at the stars."

Oscar Wilde

CELEBRATION

Jake rolls into the Four Roses with the swagger of the boy who got laid on prom night. It doesn't really matter that he just woke up in the doorway next to Tad's Steaks, to a blaring sun and garbage trucks. Pelican says "a winner acts like he's winning, especially when he's losing." Pelican always has a girl. Pelican always has money for beer.

Jake makes his way to his usual seat at the end of the bar, enduring a chorus of back slaps and sweaty palms and "hey jakes" and "where ya beens." It's only a quarter to eleven but most of the daytime regulars are here. Mickey Sue and Gene the Queen play cards over gin. Laslo sits in the corner pretending to read a book, furtively eyeing a couple of college girls leaning over the jukebox. Delores is drunk and hanging on a postman at the bar. She has a hand inside his pants, jerking him off while he nurses a beer. A lot of the postmen cash their checks at the Four Roses.

"Take it in the bathroom, Delores," barks Shelley, the bartender.

She throws Jake a wink as she pours him a Dewars on the rocks.

"This one's on me. Happy Birthday, babe."

"Thanks, Shelley. Nice of you to remember."

Jake drains his glass and starts to feel even again.
"Pelican been in?"
Shelley refills his drink.
"Nope. Haven't seen him in a few days."
She eyes him uneasily.
"Ain't seen Babs neither."

It's too early for Barbara, who works the corner at 27th street, sucking dick underneath the West Side rail. By lunchtime the cabs and delivery vans will start to circle the block. Babs is older than the other girls but she's still got great tits and will do bareback for an extra twenty. She and Jake started going together about six months ago, after Jake broke that sailor's jaw with the payphone. It was Fleet Week and everyone was buying the sailor shots at the bar—Jagermeister, tequila, and whiskey. It wasn't long before he was shit-faced and got a little rough with Babs. Jake busted him up pretty bad. Babs took Jake home that night. The payphone doesn't work anymore.

Babs keeps a room over at the Sunshine Hotel. Jake stays with her two or three nights a week. He likes how she always smells of jasmine and absentmindedly strokes his hair while she laughs at the television. It bothers him sometimes, knowing she goes with so many men. Everyone at the Four Roses gives him shit about Barbara. Everyone except Pelican, who just smiles and says "Everyone has to suck a little dick now and then." All Jake knows is that Babs ain't been nothing but kind to him, especially that time he got so sick and even after he lost his job at the garage. Babs says if she has a good night, she's gonna get them a room at the Holiday Inn, so they can celebrate Jake's birthday properly. She says they've got big bathtubs over there. And room service.

By nine o'clock, the Four Roses is jammed with whores and winos, salesmen and tranny-chasers, coked-up cabbies and sanitation workers, junky musicians and he-shes, and those artsy college kids who like to drink dollar cans of beer and feel gritty. But Jake doesn't mind them. Word is out that it's his birthday and he is high on whiskey. Street Fighting Man blares from the jukebox and Jake is dancing with Delores and Wanda of the Ukraine. It's been years since Jake has danced. He hoots and hollers as raises his arms in the air, pumping a fist in rhythm to the music.

"It's my birthday," he shouts, "It's my birthday!"

Pelican arrives in a gray linen suit, a wilted carnation stuffed into his lapel. His long white hair is streaked yellow with nicotine stains. He keeps it slicked back beneath a white fedora and carries an ornate wooden cane he claims to have acquired in Mongolia in payment of a gambling debt.

"They've got this weird kind of polo there, Jack!" Pelican calls everybody "Jack."

He finds a stool and hangs his cane on the bar. He grins at Shelley. He has a wide smile, full of teeth, like James Coburn.

"Jameson. Neat. And get me a short beer too, won't you, doll?"

Shelley eyes Pelican coolly. She doesn't like his smile and the disgusting folds of skin that hang beneath his chin and which earned him the nickname, "Pelican." She has heard his Mongolian cane story a hundred times and of his years spent as a smuggler of antiquities, and how he used to run a brothel in the Philippines and prospect for gold in Mexico. Shelley thinks Pelican is full of shit. Her aunt knows this guy that went to high school with Pelican. She says he used to sell insurance and he was once really fat. Then his wife left him and he started doing lots of coke, although nobody knows which came first. After a couple of heart attacks, Pelican got really skinny and now he's got those stupid jowls. Pelican makes Shelley want to puke. Still, her mom always said "if you ain't got nothing nice to say, it's best to keep your mouth shut." Shelley pours him a shot and leaves to get his beer.

Jake returns to the bar and takes a seat beside Pelican.

"I'm glad you came. You've been missing the party."

"Sorry, Jack. I've got some clients in from Hong Kong. You know how that is."

"Sure, Pelican, I know. I was just getting worried you'd miss all the fun, that's all."

"I'm here, aren't I?"

Pelican gives Jake a friendly slap on the back as Shelley returns with his beer.

"Jack's next round is on me. Today is his birthday."

Jake cackles, feeling his whiskey.

"Damn straight."

Shelley snickers as she walks off.

Pelican pulls a twenty from his pocket and presses it into Jake's hand. He leans over and whispers into his ear.

"Get yourself a room at the Liberty tonight, Jack. No buddy of mine is going to be sleeping in the street on his birthday."

"Thanks, Pelican. You're a real friend and I appreciate it." Jake places the money on the bar.

"But I don't need it. Babs is getting us a room at the Holiday Inn."

Jake is beaming with pride. Pelican sighs.

"About that. I'm sorry but I kind of need Barbara tonight."

"What do you mean?"

"These clients...from Hong Kong. It's good money for her, Jack."

Jake nods as he bites his lower lip, trying to mask his disappointment.

"So Babs isn't coming at all?"

"I'm afraid not."

Shelley returns with Jake's whiskey. He downs it in a single gulp. Pelican laughs as he gets up from his seat and takes his cane off the bar.

"Take it easy, Tiger. You've got the whole night ahead of you."

Pelican slaps Jake on the shoulder and smiles. All teeth.

"Happy Birthday, Jack."

Jake watches glumly as Pelican exits the bar. He looks down at the bar to see Pelican's twenty dollar bill still sitting there. He slides it over to Shelley.

"Thanks for taking such good care of me tonight."

Shelley looks at him skeptically.

"Don't you need that, babe?"

Jake shrugs his shoulders.

"I'm at the Four Roses with all my friends. What else could I need?"

Shelley places her hand over Jake's and gives it a gentle squeeze.

"Thanks. And I'm sorry your plans didn't work out."

Shelley smiles as tilts her head toward the rear of the bar.

"There's always Delores."

Jake looks over to see a crowd of people gathered around Delores, clapping their hands. She has taken off her blouse and is dancing in her bra. A string of fake pearls hangs from her neck. Delores spins around in circles as the crowd cheers her on. She notices Jake watching her from the bar and gestures for him to join her.

"It's my birthday too, Jake! It's my birthday too!"

Jake laughs so hard that he begins to cry.

"Happy birthday, Delores!" he shouts. "Happy Birthday!"

BILLY'S TOPLESS

Arnie slips a couple of dollars into her garter and waits for the big reveal. Sheila flashes a smile through wisps of frizzy red hair and slowly pulls down her g-string, offering Arnie a peek at his prize.

"No good," thinks Arnie. Another shaved pussy.

Arnie hates shaved pussies. They depress the shit out of him. Seeing a bald pussy reminds him of his ex-wife. After 8 years of marriage, Gina had suddenly shaved her pussy. It wasn't initiated by Arnie. Hell, they had never even spoken of such a thing. But on the morning of March 18, 1992, while Arnie was brushing his teeth, he saw his wife's reflection as she stepped out of the shower, her cunt freshly shaven. It was then he knew she was having an affair.

It wasn't much of a confrontation. Gina confessed readily and didn't seem too broken up about it. She moved out the next day. She got remarried a couple of years later to some lawyer in Katonah. Arnie heard her house has seven bathrooms. He wonders if Gina still shaves her pussy. He imagines her doing it in a different bathroom each day of the week.

Arnie offers Sheila a polite smile, then gets up from his seat and heads to the bar. He orders another Seven and Seven. He feels a little bad about walking away like that. She had a nice looking pussy for sure, thin-lipped and pink, and opening just enough to make him imagine a different life. Arnie thinks about inviting her to have a drink with him after her set. Maybe he should apologize for being such a prick and explain that even though she has a pussy like a cheshire smile, he just can't get past how naked it is. Another dumb idea. He knows better than to think Sheila gives a rat's ass about what he thinks of her cunt.

She has moved on anyway, shaking her ass to "Taking Care of Business," for Teddy, one of Billy's regulars. The girls all call him "White Wine," because of his ashen complexion and his habitual drink, Chardonnay on the rocks. Teddy jumps up from his seat, spilling his wine as he hoots and hollers at her tremendous ass, cheering Sheila on as if she were in a prizefight.

"Oh yeah! You got it, baby."

Teddy turns to the bar to share his admiration for Sheila, shouting at no one in particular as he pimp-walks back and forth in front of the stage.

"She's the one. You know it."

Some of the other patrons begin to toss dollar bills onto the stage. As the music ends, Sheila collects her money and heads for the ladies' room. Teddy pulls a comb from his pocket and runs it through his long, greasy hair, anxious for her return.

Arnie watches as a new girl takes the stage, dressed in a string bikini and high heels. She has long black hair, thick eyebrows, and olive skin. He thinks she must be Greek.

"I bet she's got quite a bush," he wonders, as he makes change for singles with the bartender.

PARIS FOR AVENUE C

Love bloomed among torn acetylene bags,
clogged needles and ashes from cigarettes.
The carnage of our addiction.

We hung it proudly on blood-spattered walls
and watched through nicotine glass,
as billy clubs beat on street punks
and forgotten tenements crumbled,
brick by brick.

We shivered in doorways waiting to cop,
too sick to sleep
or eat
or fuck
but flush with cash,
stolen from careless purses
or given willingly by old queens,
hungry for dick.

And when we swore each time would be the last,
I knew it was a lie.
For when I looked at you,
I saw porcelain skin for track marks
and the gardens of Paris for dopamine eyes.
We were not ghosts wrapped in sallow paper
but lovers with perfect breasts and eager hearts
draped in satin sheets
and serenaded by the drunks of Avenue C.

THE INTERNATIONAL BAR

Nancy rolls into the International
a beret over grimy hair
"I just came from home" she says
and Shelley smiles and pours
two fingers of Old Crow
as always for Nancy
who she passes every afternoon
passed out in doorways
with gray skin and shopping bags
stuffed with clothes

Jake has saved Nancy
a seat at the bar
same one every day
as if they were in love
but they rarely speak
except to hold hands
in cold comfort or desperation
as they wait for night
and the inevitable disappointment
that dawn brings

And Alex the Queen has got money
in the juke and it's always X
she plays until Black Mark screams
"SHAT UP WIT YA PHONY PINK HAIR"
but he never leaves his stool
cause he's working on his book

and everyone knows she carries a .38
nobody knows how to treat a lady
she says besides he's too busy
waiting for inspiration.

Columbian Eric comes in with Lola the dog
and all the junkies come to life
beady eyes on sallow skin
but he ain't holding
and Mena begins to cry
cause she's dopesick and pregnant
and gives head in the bathroom
for only 10 dollars a pop
"Maybe later" says Eric and Lola
licks the tears from Mena's cheek.

Then Pirate Tom calls on the payphone
he left 3 hours ago
to score some coke
"WHERE YA BEEN" says Shelley
tired of always waiting on him
"FUCK" she says "Tommy's in the tombs"
and she holds up the receiver
so he can hear them all
laugh and howl
into the night.

THE BEGINNING OF HISTORY

Sometimes Kenny's father takes him into the city on a Saturday afternoon. He never seems to have a particular destination in mind. They drive around the perimeter of Central Park and up into Harlem as the old man rattles on about Woody Allen and jazz music, and how much he wishes he never gave up his seventy-nine dollar-a-month rent-controlled apartment for that shit-box on Long Island. Kenny has no idea what he does for a living but Kenny knows that his father is always broke. He wonders if that's why his father doesn't always show up on Saturday afternoons.

"There's the Museum of Natural History," he says in a cloud of cigarette smoke. "They got a whale in there that hangs from the ceiling."

Kenny's eyes grow wide as he imagines the great fish suspended in the air. He takes in the giant building as they pass, a palace of stone. Crowds of people are gathered on the steps leading up to the entrance of the museum--pretty girls in sundresses sit with knees pressed together, smiling for their boyfriends' cameras, while mothers drag reluctant sons to the door by their shirt collars. They hold hotdogs and steaming pretzels in their hands, their fingers stained with mustard.

Kenny has never been to the museum. He knows the old man will never take him. For all the times they have driven into the city on a Saturday afternoon, he has never been to a museum or the circus or any of the places that fathers take their sons. Kenny quietly assembles a list in his head of all the places he'd like to go: Yankee Stadium; the Hayden Planetarium; the Empire State Building; and that museum with the giant whale that hangs from the ceiling, slowly disappearing from view in the rear window of the Gran Torino.

After a while, they make their way downtown. The old man parks, as he always does, in front of a luncheonette that sits beneath the abandoned High Line. Several men stand outside the store, drinking coffee and smoking cigarettes. They greet Kenny's dad with excited shouts, cracking jokes and swearing and shoving one another playfully. Kenny likes their loud voices and unshaven faces. He wonders how his father met these men, who seem so familiar with him.

They step inside the restaurant and take two seats at the counter. Fat Greek sits on a stool by the cash register, watching the Mets on a small television that hangs on the wall. Kenny doesn't know why they call him that--he doesn't look fat to Kenny--but the Greek doesn't seem to mind. He smiles at Kenny as he makes him a Cherry Lime Rickey and talks baseball with the old man. Kenny's father orders them a couple of cheeseburgers. Kenny looks forward to the luncheonette. He loves the sweet, syrupy drinks and the thickness of the french fries, and how the walls are decorated with pictures of baseball players clipped from newspapers. All of the photographs are of sports figures, except for one framed picture of JFK that hangs over the cash register. The frame is surrounded by dollar bills that have been taped to the wall.

Kenny eats half of the cheeseburger then slides off his stool, heading for the door.

"Don't wander too far," his father says, his eyes never leaving the baseball game.

Kenny steps outside, looking up and down the street. The loud, burly men have left. He walks to the corner, eyeing the stairs leading up to the abandoned railway above. His father took him up there once to show him the train tracks. They found an old railroad spike that Kenny keeps in an old cigar box underneath his bed. He climbs the steps. The entrance has long been fenced off but Kenny sees where the chain-link has been cut and pulled away from the posts. He squeezes through the fence and onto the platform. There is garbage scattered everywhere. He walks along the rails for a couple of blocks, an overgrown garden of lifeless, brown weeds and broken glass. The ground is littered with hypodermic needles and dried up condoms. He pokes at them with a stick as he looks for bottle caps and smooth pieces of shale, filling his pockets with only the best stones.

Kenny reaches the railing of the platform, which overlooks the street. Several women stand on the sidewalk below. They wear tight dresses and skirts so short that Kenny can see their underwear. Others are dressed only in t-shirts and thongs. They wave to the cars as they pass, squeezing their breasts as they shout to the drivers. A red Monte Carlo pulls over to the curb. One of the women approaches the car and leans into the open window. She is talking to the driver but Kenny can't hear what she is saying. Her skirt barely covers her ass, which is so smooth and brown that it makes Kenny think of caramel. He watches intently as she shifts her weight from one leg to the other. She has beautiful legs, long and thick. Kenny's breath begins to quicken.

She runs around the car to the passenger-side and gets in. From up on the platform, Kenny cannot see their faces but he watches as the driver gives the woman some money and unbuckles his pants. She leans over the driver, pulling down her bra to reveal her breasts. Her nipples are almost black in color. He plays with them roughly as he frees his dick from his pants. The woman quickly slides a condom down over his cock and takes him into her mouth. Kenny watches the woman's head as it bobs up and down over his lap, and the driver's fist, as it tightens around the steering wheel. Kenny's heart begins to pound in his chest as a warmth grows between his legs.

"Kenny! Where the fuck are you, kid?"
The old man's voice startles Kenny. He turns to see his father in the distance, standing on the platform. Flustered, Kenny runs to him.

"What are you doing down there?" his father asks suspiciously.

Kenny is flushed. He walks past him, toward the stairs.

"Looking for rocks," he mumbles.

"Rocks? What can you do with rocks?"

They drive back to Long Island in silence. Kenny looks out the window, avoiding his father's gaze as the urban landscape slowly dissolves into green grass and split-level ranches. His father eyes him curiously.

"Did you have fun today?"

Kenny shrugs.

"Maybe next time we'll go to a Mets game."

JUNKIE LIKE ME

A small trickle of blood ran down Rachel's forearm as Kenny pulled the needle from her vein. He wiped it away with his t-shirt and gently laid her back on the sagging sofa. He wiped her long bangs away from her eyes and gently stroked her cheek. She was gone. Usually, she would babble incoherently for a while before nodding out but this shit was strong. Rachel had copped at a new spot, Clinton Bomber. New dope brands were never stronger than they were the first couple of weeks after they hit the street. Word of mouth was everything. Depending on the frequency of his habit, a bag of new dope could keep a junkie straight for two or three days, while he might need a bag a day of an established brand. Once the word spread, however, and a new brand got a following, the dealers would cut it down to increase profits. Kenny wished they could have gotten more.

He fished through Rachel's pockets until he found the bag of speed. Over the last few days, Kenny had been trying to reduce his dope habit by shooting more and more speed. He grabbed Rachel's needle and spoon, and walked down the hall to the bathroom. Locking the door behind him, he went to work cleaning Rachel's works, which were clogged with dried blood. When he finished, he cooked up the bag of speed in the spoon. Usually, he would only do half a bag or mix a speed ball with some dope. Today he just wanted a rush.

He found a vein quickly. He always did. He pulled back on the plunger, drawing a little blood into the chamber, then pushed the speed into his vein. Within seconds his body began to shake violently and his vision started to blur. Kenny had never had a seizure before but he imagined this is what one felt like. He felt like he was being jack-hammered between two worlds. He started to scream as he fell into the bathroom door, convinced he was going to die.

Kenny didn't die. He awoke some time later to the sound of Rachel banging on the bathroom door. His chin was covered in dried snot and saliva and his head was pounding something fierce. If there had been anything in his stomach at all, he was sure he would puke. He unlocked the door and Rachel stuck her head in.

"Shit, Kenny. What the fuck have you been doing in here?"

"I shot too much speed. I think I just had a seizure."

Rachel pushed open the door and sat down on the floor beside Kenny. She hugged him close.

"You okay?" she asked.

"I guess so. Didn't you hear me screaming?"

"Shit, I was out, babe. But Eric's been home all afternoon."

Eric was their roommate, who lived in the downstairs bedroom of their duplex. Rachel was right. He would have heard Kenny. Maybe he just imagined he had screamed. Maybe he did scream but no sound could escape his body.

Rachel wadded up some toilet paper and wet it in the

sink. She gently washed his face and wiped the dried blood from his forearm. Rachel wasn't the nurturing type but Kenny enjoyed those rare moments when she mothered him. She got him up to his feet.

"C'mon," she said. "Your dad's downstairs."

Kenny looked at her incredulously. Rachel shrugged her shoulders.

"He said he needed to talk to you."

"Come with," Kenny muttered.

Rachel shook her head. Kenny couldn't blame her. His family despised her, convinced she had turned him into an addict. The Devil Woman. Of course, this wasn't true. He had embraced his addiction happily. Indeed, he had rushed to it without hesitation, tossing everything aside that stood in his way—his fiancée, his friends, and his career.

"Is there any speed left?"

Kenny didn't need to answer. Annoyed, Rachel returned to their bedroom.

Kenny entered the living room to find his dad sitting on the couch. He took a chair on the opposite side of the room, suddenly aware of how expansive it was. He and his roommates never used the living room. His dad was swallowed up by it. Kenny had not seen him in several years. He had put on some weight and his hair had turned grey, except for his moustache, which was stained yellow from nicotine. His dad crossed the room and offered Kenny a Winston. Kenny lit one up. The hot smoke felt good in his lungs. Kenny had switched to Kools months ago. Something about the menthol smoke made it easier to cope with the near constant dope-sickness. It had been a while since he had smoked a real cigarette and he was enjoying the dense flavor of the Winston.

His dad sat down on the coffee table opposite him.

"Your mom told me you're moving to Texas."

"Can't stay here. They'll put me back in jail."

His dad nodded appreciatively.

"Did I ever tell you that I was addicted to heroin once?"

As soon as he heard the words, Kenny knew they weren't true.

"No, dad. You never mentioned that."

"Yeah, when I was your age…"

He seemed to take a beat for dramatic effect.

"I was worried I might be gay. So I started shooting heroin."

Kenny had often wondered if his dad was gay but still found the story incredible.

"Wow."

"Yeah," his dad said as his chest swelled, "I used to shoot it behind my knee, so no one would see my track marks."

"How did you quit?"

"Cold turkey. With the help of a local priest."

Kenny tried to imagine his Bronx Jew of a dad, confiding in some priest that he was a gay heroin addict. No. This was pretty weak. Even for his dad.

"And no one in the family knew about it?," Kenny asked.

"Just your Uncle Herb."

The thought of Uncle Herb made Kenny smile. He was the family pothead and Kenny used to smoke joints with him when he was a teenager. He only addressed him as "Uncle Herb"—with a silent "H." His dad took Kenny by the hand.

"When Uncle Herb went to see you in the prison last month, he came to me afterwards and said, 'I can't believe it's happening again.' You see, I was just like you."

Kenny thought this was a nice touch. Part of him wanted the story to be true, as if his deterioration could be traced back to some latent family defect. Of course, his dad seemed to be forgetting that Kenny had been adopted.

"I wish you could stay with me but it's just not possible. Why don't you stay with your mother? She'll take you in."

"What about Rachel?," Kenny asked.

His dad shrugged his shoulders. Kenny pulled his hand from his father's grasp and stood up.

"Thanks for coming by, dad."

Kenny walked out of the room and climbed the stairs. He wondered if Rachel had any dope left.

THIS CITY IS A DRUNKEN MOTHER

this city is a drunken mother
shouting at you
with blaring horns
and broken glass
eyes full of murder
and indifference
while you suck cock
under the C-yard
fondled by anxious queens
with wrinkled currency

this city is an absent father
masturbating
in mirrored rooms
and penthouse suites
nostrils full of coke
and resentment
their naked disappointment
in all that you dream
and the promise of youth

this city is an abandoned child
veins full of junk
like asphalt in potholes
wandering from
bed to bed
where lovers wait
in soiled sheets
as callous as
their mothers and fathers

SWEET BIRD OF YOUTH
(OR I'M SORRY, TENNESSEE)

they run in the streets
knives drawn
eager for bread and love
as the mad poet said
a man they never knew
so fuck him
they are dressed for sex
they are dressed for murder
waiting impatiently
to go viral

you shake your head
you shrug your shoulders
standing on the curb
derision as old and yellow
as nicotine fingers
and undershirts
stained with sweat
you are dead to them
dead as the mad poet
they never knew

so fuck you too

JAMBALAYA AND NEGLIGEE

Ann kept her second husband's ashes in a ceramic vase by the door and for dinner, liked to serve jambalaya over spaghetti instead of rice. Born and raised in Turtle Creek, she wept often over the loss of her fortune and her late husband Edgar's demise. Once while driving in her car on Easter Sunday, she burst into tears as we passed a church, declaring "this is the day they killed Jesus." I didn't have the heart to tell her the good man had been hung up days before. For all of her idiosyncrasies, Ann was the only one in Leslie's family willing to take us in—two, homeless junkies fleeing from prosecution. Besides, I didn't give a shit about Jesus.

The trip from New York to Dallas took 36 hours, most of it spent huddled with Leslie in the back of a bus, shivering and dope-sick under the nervous eyes of the driver. He had been suspicious of us since Memphis, where Leslie, in less than an hour, had managed to steal a passenger's purse, locate a dope spot, and score a bag of heroin. Her criminality was relentless and exhausting, her pockets a bottomless well of stolen cigarettes, chewing gum, and jewelry. The dope was sticky brown. Leslie cooked it up in a bottle-cap she found between the seat cushions, having mixed it with her own saliva. Of course the needle clogged and the dope was wasted. She spent nearly an hour on the bus toilet before finally giving up. Leslie rested her head on my shoulder and cried in frustration as I covered her with my coat.

"There's some things you should know about my mother. First, she's beautiful. Second, she's very competitive with me. She will try to seduce you. She's flirted with all of my boyfriends. Third, I'll never forgive her for not believing me when I told her Aron raped me."

Aron was Leslie's brother. Shit. Leslie had a flair for drama. I mulled that over for a while as she drifted off to sleep.

Ann picked us up in a convertible Mercedes. She had fiery red hair and dark eyes that regarded me coolly, making it quite clear that I was but a temporary nuisance in her life.

"I do hope you'll use this opportunity to get your life together."

She spoke slowly and deliberately in a lilting drawl. Still, she seemed sincere enough.

"You didn't have to get all dressed up for the bus station," Leslie quipped.

Ann had draped a single strand of pearls over a gold-colored silk blouse that offered more than a hint of cleavage. Her wrists were adorned with several gold and bejeweled bracelets, which jangled as she walked us to her car in tight designer jeans, her ass swaying rhythmically to their music.

Ann lived out in Plano in one of those gated, townhouse communities. She showed us to our bedroom and laid down the house rules:

No drugs, predictably.

We had one month to get jobs and to find an apartment.

She would help us get into a place but only if satisfied that we were clean.

It sounded pretty reasonable to me.

We slept for two days, until our sickness had subsided. On the third day, Ann treated me to my first real meal in more than a year, homemade jambalaya. It was as if I had never tasted food before. Dormant for months, all of my senses now seemed amplified, detecting every spice, every nuance of the dish she had served. Fortified and rested, I began searching for a job. Within a week, I landed a gig at the Dallas Museum of Art. Ann was impressed and slowly her estimation of me began to improve.

Free from dope for the first time in two years, my sex drive returned with a vengeance. Late one night, Leslie and I snuck out to the hot tub together. Our scarred bodies glistened in the dark, steamy water—even track marks look beautiful under moonlight. We kissed for a long time as she straddled my lap. After a while, the heat of the water got to be too much. Leslie stood up and bent over edge of the tub. She grinned at me as she raised her ass up out of the water and stretched her wiry frame across the cold mosaic tiles that lined the pool. Invigorated by her ass and the cool night air on my skin, I began to fuck her from behind. It was then that I saw Ann watching us from behind the translucent panels that covered her bedroom window. She quickly pulled back from the glass when I looked in her direction. How long had she been there? The thought of her watching us made me come.

Leslie left early the next morning to visit her Dad. I laid in bed naked and half-asleep, listening to the bumps and shuffles of Ann milling about the house. It was cleaning day. I heard her footsteps approach and a soft rap on the bedroom door. Rather than cover myself, I closed my eyes and pretended to be asleep. The door scraped gently against the carpet as Ann entered the room. I could feel her eyes on me for a long time as she stood motionless at the foot of the bed. All was quiet except for the quickening sound of her breathing. After a minute or two, she gathered our clothes from the floor and tiptoed out of the room.

Leslie began waitressing at a restaurant near Deep Ellum. Within a few weeks, we had saved up enough money for a small efficiency. It wasn't much to speak of but we were excited to have a place we could make our own. The night before we were to move out, I arrived home from work to find Ann dressed in a sheer negligee with a Vodka Collins in her hand. She had been taking an increasing amount of Xanax since our arrival in Dallas and was now stumbling about the house like some hopped-up Blanche Dubois. While her transparency saddened me, I could not help but admire her body as it moved beneath the shimmering fabric of her lingerie. She led me to the kitchen, where she had set out a bowl of her jambalaya, served over spaghetti.

"I wanted to make you something special before you left," she said.

She smiled at me flirtatiously as she placed her hand on my shoulder, her warm fingers tickling the back of my neck. I could not help but think of Edgar's ashes, sitting in a vase by the door, like a forgotten umbrella left behind by a house guest.

Leslie came home a short while later and upon seeing her mother, began to cry. We moved out the next morning.

SWAN LAKE

He found her as he always did, asleep on the toilet seat, her gaunt frame slumping forward, defying gravity—like a licorice ribbon in a child's hand. The needle dangled from her forearm, as it always did, followed by a thin stream of dried blood. She was naked but for a pair of panties that hung around her ankles, worn white cotton sullied by the cigarette ash that had fallen from her outstretched hand.

He cleaned her up as he always did, gently washing her face, now damp with perspiration, and scrubbing the blood from her scabby arms. He removed her panties and scooped up her tired body. He carried her into the bedroom and placed her on the bed. It was a cold night for Dallas and he covered her with her a patchwork quilt made by her grandmother. It was crafted from a collection of pattern samples for men's suits. It was her favorite. Half-conscious and still on the nod, she muttered incoherently as she rolled over onto her side and buried her head beneath the quilt. She often hid her face while she slept. It reminded him of how swans sleep, with their bills tucked into a folded wing.

He spent the next hour cleaning. Her daily routine left behind a trail of bloodstains, cigarette butts, candy wrappers, and dirty laundry. It was nearly midnight when he finished, so he sat in the kitchen, listening to the rattle of the washing machine as he nursed a beer. He had been lucky enough to find a crumpled pack of Kools in her jeans and was pleased to find that only few were broken. A tattered copy of the "Executioner's Song" sat on the kitchen table, so he decided to read for a while. Although he had long since memorized its most poignant passages, he frequently reread the book, enjoying the sense of accomplishment he felt each time he completed it. He smoked one cigarette after the other until all but two were gone. He left them for her on the kitchen table.

It was 2 am when he finally got into bed. Laying beside her, he thought of the lakeside cabin they had rented once in upstate New York. The water had been too cold for him but she dove right in. She loved the water the way a child loves the water, swimming for hours until their lips turn blue and their fingertips start to prune. She had always been braver than he was. Sensing him there beside her, she woke momentarily. She offered a sleepy apology as she nuzzled into him, pressing her ass against his crotch as he wrapped his arms around her. He drifted off to sleep, carried by the soft cadence of her breathing and wondering if he would ever have the strength to leave her.

RETURN TO LONG SLEEVES

It was that open package of condoms that broke him into pieces, so swiftly and completely, that Kenny sat huddled in the corner of the bedroom, like a marionette that had lost its strings. Earlier that evening, he watched Rachel slip quietly from beneath their sheets and pull on a pair of black leggings, which she wore compulsively, regardless of season. They had fucked that night for the first time in several weeks. The dope had long since robbed Rachel of her sex drive but occasionally she offered up her pussy to him out of guilt, like a dry crust of bread to an orphan. He knew the drugs were to blame but couldn't help but feel resentful about it sometimes. It had been a hard, angry fuck. He pretended not to hear when she complained he was driving too deep. Nor did he notice her wincing in pain when he pinched and twisted her nipples.

In the darkness, Kenny heard her fumbling for something in the dresser drawer.

"What are you doing?" he said sleepily.

"I'm sick. I need to cop," she said bluntly.

"Ride it out. I'll stay up with you."

She ignored him.

"You have money? How?"

Rachel slipped a t-shirt on over her head.

"My mom gave me money for some new clothes. I'll be back in a little while."

She left. He sat up, rubbing his eyes as he looked at the clock. 1 a.m. Something didn't feel right. Kenny felt guilty about making her go alone but he had been clean for 8 months now and wasn't sure if he was strong enough to hold a bag of dope in his hands. He had devoted the last several months to weaning Rachel off heroin, with mixed success. His first strategy had been to cut off her supply. He had run off most of her junkie friends and stopped giving her money. In retaliation, Rachel had sold off nearly everything they owned and had written some bad checks. They got evicted from their place on Ellsworth and they were already a few weeks behind on the rent for the new efficiency. Still, she had seemed more like her old self lately and he had convinced himself that she must be cutting back.

Kenny grumbled as he got out of bed. Her mother knew not to give her cash. What had she been fumbling with in the dresser? He opened the drawer and found them there, hidden beneath a pair of panties—an open pack of Trojans. He picked up the package. The box said it held three but there was only one left. They had never used condoms when they fucked. Junkies don't menstruate much. He knew then, how she was getting money for dope. That knowledge made him puke all over the carpet in the bedroom. After he had cleaned up the mess, he sat in the corner waiting for Rachel to return.

She returned less than an hour later with two bags of dope. He confronted her then, calling her a whore and a liar.

"I don't fuck them," she said. "I make them pay me up front for a blowjob. Once they pull their pants down,

I jump out of the car."

He desperately wanted to believe her.

"If that's true, what the fuck do you need condoms for?"

Rachel just stared at him blankly.

"Fuck off. I don't belong to you."

She went into the kitchen and cooked up her dope. He sat alone in the bedroom for a while, wondering if he really had a right to be angry. More than once, Kenny had let an old troll suck him off for drug money. He hadn't always told her about it but the money he earned was to get them both straight. Kenny always shared it with her. Still, he questioned if he would have done it if he hadn't needed to get high himself. Would he have let some stranger jerk off all over his ass if it was only Rachel that was dope sick? He wasn't so sure anymore.

He went into the kitchen where he found her crying in frustration, unable to find a vein. She had been poking herself repeatedly and thin trails of blood ran down her forearms. Kenny started to weep. Rachel lashed out at him angrily.

"This is your fucking fault. I wouldn't have to do this if you would just give me some money. You act so fucking superior now that you're clean."

He took the needle from her hand and tied her off. After a couple of tries, he was able to find a vein. Rachel raised a bloodied hand and wiped the tears from his eyes.

"Sorry."

Kenny nodded, knowing that she was.

"I bought you a bag too."

He smiled sadly, knowing she was lying once again.

"Please get high with me. Just one last time."

He eyed the bag of dope, sitting on the table, wanting

to erase the last eight months of lies and stealing and accusations and skipped meals and bus rides and shitty minimum wage jobs and emergency room visits and generic cigarettes and ninety-nine cent tacos and hiding from the landlord and beat artists that called and hung up when he answered, and the fighting, the constant fighting.

In the morning Kenny slipped quietly out of bed and pulled on his jeans. He looked at the fresh scab that now marked his forearm. Back to long sleeves. Eight months clean and he had nothing to show for it. He finished dressing and dug his backpack out of the closet. It still had the manuscript in it that he had brought with him from New York. His unfinished masterpiece. He leaned over and kissed Rachel on the forehead.

"I've got to go to work" he said.

She stirred slightly and blew a kiss in his direction before returning to her slumber.

Later that day Kenny quit his job. He waited around until they paid him what he was due and then took a bus to the airport. He called Rachel's father from a payphone and told him he was leaving. Kenny begged him to take her in. Rachel's father said he would think about it.

He arrived in New York late that evening. His father had left a blanket for him on the couch. It had been years since Kenny had stepped foot inside his father's home but it all seemed very much the same. A dusty bookshelf leaned against the wall opposite the couch, lined with baseball memorabilia and black and white photographs turned yellow from nicotine. He felt overwhelmed by the sameness of it all.

He called Rachel's father again but his wife answered the phone. She was a little drunk, as she often was. "He's at the hospital," she said coolly. "Rachel was raped tonight. When are you coming back to get her?"

PARLOUR TRICKS

The trajectory of the scars on your wrist
lead directly to your heart.
But when I try to follow you there
I am met with resistance; a villain on the road
disguised in the foul mouth of the sailor,
behind cheshire smiles and broken glass,
and under callous whiskey fingers,
trained to deliver a hand job with indifference
and roll cigarettes with the skill of a three-time loser.
Parlour tricks meant to divert me,
away from your heart
into the hothouse of your cunt.
You know it is there, that I will languish,
happy and stupid and drunk on your pussy,
full as a tick,
like a junkie on the nod.
It is always there that I lose.

PAINTED TOES

I have seen horrible and wonderful things.

I watched the angels descend on Port Authority as I shot dope in the bathroom stall and climbed the Brooklyn Bridge to scream at the stars.

I shared my methadone with Herbert Hunke, as he told me about Words.

I went to jail.

I fucked amazing, beautiful women.

One of them smelled of fresh apples in October.

Some of them even loved me.

I peddled my cock to old men in Lincoln Continentals with Jersey plates and cried at the feet of leather-clad dominas.

I dropped acid on the beach, naked under a blood orange moon.

I drove the tour bus from San Francisco to L.A., high on hashish and crazy, evangelical AM radio.

I shared cigarettes and a short beer with dive bar bums, and was chased by police down Avenue D.

I was homeless.

I was a thief.

I sang Hank Williams' songs to my daughters until they grew sleepy in my arms.

I lost friends to heroin, watching them crumble under the weight of existence, like cherry blossoms in a windstorm.

I lost friends to complacency.

I was healed by the laughter of those that survived.
I have seen horrible and wonderful things.

But I still long to see your painted toes on the dashboard
of the Plymouth, as it races along the highway, your long
tan legs kissed by the August sun.
The Blasters are on the stereo and your warm hand rests
lazily on my thigh.
Like always, there is no destination.
Just a salty breeze blowing through your cinnamon hair.

FIREFLIES

The boy knocks on the screen door. It is after seven and starting to get dark. He watches as the August fireflies dance in the tall grass. He wonders how much Mrs. Sawyer would pay him to cut the lawn.

"What do you want, ass-wipe?"

Charlie is standing at the door, a stoned grin on his face. Charlie is Timmy's older brother. He is a lanky sixteen and his face is riddled with acne.

"Is Timmy around?" the boy asks.

"He went to the 7-11. You can wait for him if you want."

Charlie turns and walks down a dark hallway toward the rear of the house. The boy watches him as he disappears into the shadows, wondering if he should follow.

He opens the screen door and enters the house. He hears the familiar march of Space Invaders on the television as he walks into the living room. Charlie sits on the couch holding a joystick. His eyes are glued to the screen. A bong sits on the coffee table.

"Can I have a hit?" the boy asks.

"Yeah, right. What are you, like ten?"

"Eleven!"

Charlie considers this for a moment, his eyes still fixed on the television.

"Nah, you'll just narc on me."

"No I won't! Stop being such a dick."

Charlie laughs as he puts down the joystick.

"Do you have any smokes?"

The boy pulls a pack of Marlboro Reds from his jeans and takes a seat on the couch beside Charlie. He offers him a cigarette, then lights up one of his own. Charlie packs a bowl and hands the bong to the boy. He takes a big hit, letting the warm smoke fill his lungs. He holds it for as long as he can before exhaling.

"Holy shit" he says.

Charlie grins.

"Thai stick."

Charlie refills the bowl for himself as the boy sinks into the couch. His entire body grows warm and numb, as if an electric blanket has been wrapped around him. The boys sit in silence for several minutes.

"Want to see something cool?" Charlie asks.

He doesn't wait for an answer. He gets up and walks out of the room.

"Can you get me a beer?" the boy shouts after him.

The boy has spent most of the summer at the Sawyer house, getting stoned and laughing at the television. Timmy's parents are rarely home.

Charlie returns with two Budweiser tall-boys and a stack of photographs in his hand. He tosses the pictures on the table.

"I found these in the attic."

The boy opens his beer and takes a long pull. It feels good on his throat, which is scratchy from the smoke. He looks through the photographs. They are all in black and white and some of them are cracked and yellowing at the edges. They mostly depict naked teenage boys and girls. Some of them look as if the photographer was peering through a window. The boy wonders whether they knew they were being photographed. One of the girls is naked in a bathtub. His cock twitches involuntarily upon seeing the photograph. The girl in the photograph resembles his classmate, Georgette Lang. He's had a crush on her since the fourth grade. The boy stares at the picture for a long time.

"Your dad is a freaking perv!"

"I guess so."

Charlie breaks into laughter. The boy takes another pull off his beer.

"Want to see something really fucked up?" asks Charlie.

"What?"

"I found a dead dog in the woods today."

"What's so special about a dead dog?" asks the boy.

"I found it in The Shed. It looks like it was sacrificed in some sort of ritual. Fucking witches, man."

"You're so full of shit!" says the boy.

Charlie gets up and walks into the kitchen. He returns with a flashlight.

"C'mon. Let's check it out."

They walk through the woods in silence, led by the moonlight and Charlie's flashlight. The boy has never liked "The Shed," a crumbling one-room shack that sits in the middle of the woods. In the winter, the older kids gather there at night to drink beer and Southern Comfort, and make out in front of a makeshift fire pit. No one knows how The Shed got to be in the middle of the woods but the boy has heard stories about a crazy old woman that used to live there. They say she liked to eat squirrels.

The boy hesitates at the entrance to the Shed but Charlie shoves him in the back, pushing him inside. The room is dark and smells rancid. Charlie turns on his flashlight. There is an old mattress in the corner and the floor is covered in broken glass and cigarette butts. Charlie aims the flashlight toward the center of the room. The dog lays on the floor, in a circle drawn in chalk. The boy moves closer and sees that its throat has been cut. Its fur is matted with dried blood and the wound filled with maggots.

"Pretty fucking sick, right?"

The boy feels vomit rising in his throat.

"I've got to take a piss," he says, before running out of the room.

The fresh air revives the boy as he stands before a tree and unzips his fly. He doesn't really have to pee but doesn't want Charlie to know how scared he is.

"You're such a little faggot," says Charlie as he appears beside the boy.

Charlie opens his jeans and starts pissing on the tree.

"I bet you've got a pussy down there, don't you?" says Charlie, staring at the boy's open fly.

"Fuck off."

"Prove it."

"What the fuck, Charlie?"

"Drop your pants. Prove that you don't have a pussy."

"I'm not dropping my pants, you asshole."

Charlie quickly grabs the boy and starts to pull down his jeans. He tries to spin free but Charlie quickly wrestles him to the ground. He straddles the boy's legs as he stares intently at his penis.

"You call that a dick? It looks like a little cunt to me."

Charlie grabs the boy's dick and yanks it violently. The boy cries out in pain.

"Cut it out, you fuck!"

Charlie grabs the boy's balls in his hand, twisting and squeezing them until the boy begins to cry.

"Please stop. You're hurting me."

Charlie begins to masturbate as he pulls on the boy's balls.

It is over in a few seconds.

Charlie stands up and closes his fly. He watches the boy threateningly as he pulls his jeans up around his hips. The boy is too scared to look him in the eye. He turns and walks away. Charlie calls after him.

"If you tell anyone about this, I'll kill your fucking dog."

The boy begins to run, Charlie Sawyer's come dripping down his thigh. He doesn't stop running until he gets home.

Two weeks later, the Sawyer home burned to the ground. No one was hurt but it was assumed that Charlie, stoned, fell asleep on the couch with a lit cigarette in his hand. The Sawyers moved away after that. The boy never told anyone about what had happened in the woods with Charlie. He was too scared he would find his dog in The Shed.

OKLAHOMA ROSE

Riding came easily to Travis. His mother said it was a gift to be at such ease with an animal and to move so effortlessly with its rhythms, like a dandelion parachute that rolls in the breeze. Even when he was a baby, she took him riding with her every morning, through the groves of dogwood and redbud that neighbored her father's ranch. Travis would sit nestled between her legs, his hands wrapped tightly around the horn of the saddle and his toes burrowing into the chestnut coat of his mother's horse. He especially liked riding with her in the spring, when the trees would shed blossoms red, purple, and white, and his mother's spirits would be lifted enough to sing to him.

By the time he was 3 he could sit atop a horse by himself, so his mother gifted him her favorite mare, Oklahoma Rose. His grandfather even built Travis a special platform, so he could climb in and out of the saddle unassisted. Travis would ride around the corral for hours at a time, while his mother watched from the porch, laughing and clapping her hands in delight.

For his fifth birthday, Travis's grandfather took him to Tulsa to see the rodeo. He marveled at the Bronc and Bull riders—the way they kept their balance astride the fury of the bucking animals—and was amazed by the precision of the calf-ropers. Travis knew then and there that he wanted to be a rodeo star. His grandfather bought him a souvenir program to encourage him and the next day, gave Travis his first roping lesson. By the time he was six, he could lasso a fence post from 15 feet away. It didn't take long before word got around about the boy-cowboy, who could ride and rope better than most men three times his age. Strangers would show up at the ranch at all hours of the day, asking to see Travis ride. His grandfather half-joked that they should sell tickets but Travis's mother wouldn't hear of it. In her view, his talents were a blessing to be shared and it wouldn't be right to charge a fee just to watch him ride a horse and swing a rope.

Travis's grandfather died that winter. His truck fell on him while he was changing the oil. The jack had slipped on the ice. Travis was only seven years old and didn't know much about death but it seemed to him his grandfather deserved a better passing than that. His mother said it was a random stupid act and for the first and only time in his life, Travis heard his mother question the existence of god. Four months later, the cancer took his mother and Travis knew she had been right.

Travis met his father for the first time at his mother's funeral. The only thing Travis knew about him was that he had served in Vietnam and had spent the last few years in California. He had dark wild hair that hung in his eyes and he smelled of tobacco and beer. He stood beside Travis at his mother's grave and helped him shovel some dirt on her coffin. And when Travis started to cry he told him to "Buck up and be a man." He drove Travis home after the funeral, where he announced he would be moving in to take care of the boy. Apparently, his parents had never bothered to divorce and with the death of Travis's grandfather and mother, the ranch belonged to his father.

Travis's father didn't have much interest in ranching. He spent most of the time out on the front porch, drinking beer and playing poker with his friends. At night, the whores would come out to the house, with heavy drawls and perfume. His father would send Travis up to his room while he fucked them in the parlor. Travis was thankful his father had the decency not to do it in his mother's bed, even if he occasionally paid them with pieces of her jewelry or one of her fancy dresses.

His military pension wasn't enough to support his drinking and gambling, so as the months passed, Travis's father sold off parcels of land and most of the livestock. He let Travis keep Oklahoma Rose, along with a couple of older horses he couldn't sell. Travis's riding was a constant source of amusement to his father. Late at night, when he was liquored up, he would pull Travis out of bed by the hair and drag him out to the porch in his underwear.

"Do some of your horse tricks, boy."

Travis didn't dare refuse. The few times he had, his father had whipped him with his belt. So Travis would climb onto the back of Oklahoma Rose and gallop back and forth in front of the porch, amidst the laughter of his father's drunken friends and prostitutes.

For Travis's eighth birthday, his father hung a sign at the entrance to the ranch.

Come See The Amazing Cow-Baby! Watch Him Rope and Ride! Only 50 Cents!

"I ain't no baby," said Travis.

His father just laughed. In the weeks that followed, Travis found himself riding at all hours of the day, for the entertainment of locals and tourists alike–anyone who was willing to pay the admission fee. His father always made him ride in his underwear.

"It makes you look younger," he said.

One family from New York was so impressed by Travis, they tipped him five dollars. His father pocketed the money.

"It's best to let me hold that for you, son."

Over time, Travis forgot all about being a rodeo star. While he would on occasion, thumb through the souvenir program his grandfather had bought him, it no longer held the magic for him that it once did.

On a cool night in April, Travis's father, drunk on whiskey

and beer, wakes him from a deep sleep with a yank on his arm.

"We got company, boy. Get your ass down there. I got your horse all saddled up for you."

"I'm tired. I don't want to ride tonight."

His father smacks him hard across the face.

"Next time it'll be my fist."

Travis hurries downstairs and out to the porch. A man and two women are seated at the picnic table, which is littered with empty beer cans. The man smirks at him.

"I ain't never seen a cowboy in tighty-whities before."

The women start to laugh. Travis's father emerges from the house. He nods toward Oklahoma Rose, who is tied up in the corral.

"Get on it, boy."

"Please, sir. I'm tired and it's cold."

One of the woman interjects.

"At least let him put on some pants, Ernie."

"Shut your hole, Lorraine. He's my boy."

Travis's father takes a step toward him threateningly.

"You ain't your mother, you know. You have to work if you want to keep living here."

"I ain't riding," Travis says.

His father stares at him for a long moment before responding.

"We'll see about that," he says with an icy stare.

Travis' father goes into the house, only to return a few minutes later with a rifle in his hand. He brings the gun to his shoulder, setting his sites on Oklahoma Rose. Travis cries out as a single shot is fired. The horse drops quickly, it was a clean kill shot to its head. Travis runs to his horse but it is already dead. It lies there in the dirt, motionless, its eyes wide open.

"I think it's time to call it a night," says one of the woman.

"Nobody's going anywhere," says Travis's father, "until the boy does his show."

He yells to Travis from the porch.

"Go saddle up a horse, son, or I'll shoot them all, one-by-one."

Travis nods as he rises to his feet and walks toward the barn.

His father turns to his friends.

"Let's all have another drink."

The tension evaporates with a few shots of whiskey and soon the friends are laughing again. It's as if no one even notices the dead horse lying in the corral. Travis emerges from the barn on an old grey steed, he gallops past the porch, turning himself full circle in the saddle as he rides.

"I ain't never seen an eight-year old ride like that," says the man.

The guest begin to cheer as Travis begins to double-back for another pass. His father shouts after him.

"Show them some of your lasso tricks, boy."

Travis's father turns to the women.

"He's a wonder with a rope. Just like his old man," he says with a wink and a cackle.

Travis reaches for his lariat as he gallops toward the porch. When he gets within ten feet, he throws his rope. It lands on target, dropping over his father's head and around his neck. Travis yanks the lariat closed, while wrapping the end of the rope around the saddle horn. It happens so quickly and with such precision, that Travis's father is still laughing as his body is suddenly pulled from the porch, his neck snapping before he hits the ground. The horse keeps running, dragging the body across the dirt. Travis guides the horse toward woods, galloping through the groves of dogwood and redbud that he once rode with his mother.

LOVE LETTER FOR KATELAN

you are the ghost that whispers in my ear
words as old as the soil
sharpened by the tongues of poets
and the rusted works
of lunatic asylums

only they understood
the power of virus
to ensnare our hearts
thrilling cock and cunt alike
moving in rhythm
with Mingus
and ancient trees
and butterfly wings
bending in a breeze
as hot as your breath
on a cheek that burns
for every word

you are the ghost that paints pictures on my skin
drawn in glitter and
sequins and menstrual blood
in tangled sheets
soiled with longing

and if I dare to dream
as the dead poets did

I can feel the earth
beneath our bare feet
ashes and bits of bone
and seashell
that carry mystery
as timeless
and beautiful
as your eyes
and the words you whisper in my ear
and the pictures you paint on my skin

DROWNING BY THE FIRE

I lie by the fire as the moon drowns the sun,
unsure of the day or even the hour.
The clocks are as dead as bits of polished wood and brass
spit out by the ocean with old photographs and songs,
memories once warmed by summer.

I imagine each moment with you as a measure in time,
a step from the shower,
ringlets of crimson hair
leave drops of water on the small of your back.
I pull you down into bed and drink them up
with a tongue saltier than the sea
and twice as hungry.

No skin can taste sweeter than that
beneath your outstretched arms,
pulled tight by my hand
and bruised by my teeth.
A canvas that turns from pink to red,
then purple to black,
a sailor puts ink to bone.

And thighs that only whispered promise,
open gladly to fingers, slick with wanting
and feed me until your body quakes
and your cunt swallows the night whole.

This is how I pass each hour of the storm,
when the clocks are as dead as bits of polished wood
and brass.

NOR'EASTER

I will strip you of your clothes
like an autumn wind robs the leaves from a tree
and my mouth will roll over your limbs
until you abandon your roots
uncertain.

And I will burrow into your flesh
as a worm, in fear of flood, turns the soil
a tongue feasting for winter's forage
until your skin turns crimson and gold
in protest.

My hand will strike your blushing cheeks
like the ocean crashes on November shores
with sailor lips I'll taste the salt on your skin
coaxing the whale upon your shoulder
into song.

SECOND STOREY WINDOW

We met at a junior high school make-out party in the basement of the Miller house. They were alcoholics who let us drink their beer in exchange for the occasional ass-grab by Mr. Miller or the cloying advances of his wife, who despite her advanced years was simply unable to prevent her bathrobe from falling open whenever Robby had his friends over. The basement was dark and cavernous, the only light sources being Robby's black light and a novelty beer sign that hung on the wall behind the bar. It was supposed to read "Miller" but the "M" had long-since burnt out.

Everyone had paired off but us. Robby had put on Black Sabbath Volume IV, which failed to drown out the moans and hushed promises that emanated from the shadows. The black light had cast a purple glow over the room, offering flashes of panty and iridescent hands that snaked effortlessly beneath halter tops and tight denim. We stared uncomfortably at one another from our beanbag chairs, trying to avert our eyes from the giant, radioactive dry-hump, whose only apparent purpose was to remind us that we were the only ones not participating.

You were 14 and the homely girl. I was 13 and overweight. I offered you a Marlboro Red and you declined. So, I asked if you wanted to "go out with me."

This time, you said "yes" and gave me a weak smile. We held hands for the rest of the night but barely spoke a word. The next day, you broke up with me. This message was delivered to me by your best friend Linda Bonetti. She wasn't very sympathetic but had really big tits.

Two years later, you had blossomed into a beautiful girl and were dating my best friend, Steve. I was still fat. One summer night, I climbed the tree next to your house and scrambled onto the roof of your garage. I slowly made my way to the ledge outside your bathroom window. The light was on. It was a warm night and the window was open. The curtains flapped gently in the breeze, providing a glimpse into the bathroom.

You had just stepped out of the shower and were rubbing moisturizer on your body. Your back was to me but in the mirror's reflection, I could see the rich, dark hair curling above your pussy. It was the most wonderful thing I had ever seen. I lost my footing for a moment. You must have heard my sneakers scraping against the roof because within seconds, you were at the window and staring right at me. I scuttled away and quickly climbed down the tree to your driveway below. I ran all the way home. Terrified, I sat in my bedroom, waiting for the police to come and take me away, waiting for a phone call that never came.

The next day, Steve came by and asked if I had been "peeping" in your window. I confessed but he didn't seem to mind all that much. A few weeks later, you sat next to me on the bus and didn't say a word about it. We talked about Blondie instead. Your favorite song was "Rip Her To Shreds." In the weeks that followed, we became friends. Not once did you ever mention seeing me outside your window.

One day, you invited me over after school. It felt strange being inside your house. We smoked a joint and drank shots of Jagermeister while we listened to the New York Dolls. Later, you stood at the sink cleaning shot glasses, complaining that Steve always got mad at you when you played punk rock. Your back was turned to me and you were wearing purple jogging shorts and a tube top. You had beautiful, sloping shoulders and the longest legs I had ever seen. That's when you mentioned it.

"I saw you that night…outside my window," you said without looking at me.

"I know." My heart was racing. You laughed.

"You're a pervert, you know that?"

"Yes."

"It's okay."

I moved over to the sink and stood behind you. Our bodies were almost touching.

"You're standing pretty close, aren't you?"

I leaned in and kissed the back of your neck as I wrapped my arms around your waist. You moaned softly and turned your head so my tongue could find yours. Your mouth tasted of warm licorice. I ran my hands over your body as we kissed, rubbing your pussy through your shorts. We kissed for a few moments before you pulled away.

"We should stop. My sister will be home from school soon."

You grabbed a couple of beers from the refrigerator and we sat at the kitchen table. We talked about school for a while, until the awkward feeling had dissipated.

We remained friends but you never invited me over again. I moved away after high school. You moved to Connecticut and married a cop. Sometimes when I walk the street at night, I'll look up at an apartment building and see a light shining from a second-storey window. I think of you then, remembering your Jagermeister lips and the dark folds of your pubic hair.

SNOW ANGELS

In December of 1982, I threw my stepfather into a wall for calling my mom "a filthy cunt." My mother was a school teacher who had raised me on her own while putting herself through school. I never thought she was filthy or a cunt. She did, however, throw me out of the house for pushing her husband's fat ass through the wall. It made a big hole in the sheet rock the size and shape of a beer keg. This sort of thing happened periodically. Her job paid more than his, so to compensate, he never missed an opportunity to insult or berate her. Consequently, I had been thrown out of the house 7 times by the age of 16. I never really questioned why she didn't take my side. It was her third marriage. The first marriage taught her to be a victim. The second taught her to be stupid. By the third marriage, she had forgotten she had ever been anything else. Marriage makes people forget things.

When I wasn't living in my mother's house, I stayed with my best friend, Pete. His parents were a pair of affable alcoholics, who were more than happy to let me sleep on their couch in exchange for the occasional bottle of vodka. Pete was still in high school. I had graduated a few months earlier and was working the night shift at a local nursing home. I spent my nights mopping up shit and blood, and mashed peas that had been thrown to the floor in futile acts of rebellion. On slow nights, I popped speed with the nurses. They flirted with me constantly. Sometimes they would fuck me too. One of them liked to drag me into a vacant room during her break. I would bend her over a hospital bed that had been stripped of its sheets and we would fuck hard and fast, trying to forget that hours earlier, someone had died there. In the corner would sit a box, filled with afghans and picture frames. I loved that job. I liked talking with the old people. I would smoke cigarettes with them before they went to bed and listen to their stories. During my breaks I would sit in the cafeteria and write. There was never a boss around to hassle me. My supervisor came in at 7 a.m. and so long as the floors were clean, she was happy.

It was the perfect job for a 16 year-old who had no idea what he wanted to do with his life. The arrangement worked well for Pete's family. As I worked nights, I was usually only around in the mornings, when his parents were at work. On my days off, we would watch James Bond movies and get drunk together. Pete's dad was a disbarred attorney who wrote legal textbooks and drank Vodka and Tab religiously. His mom worked in the accounting department of a local hospital. When she drank, which was often, she always wore a powder-blue, terrycloth robe and yellow knee socks. I rarely saw her dressed in anything else. Pete called it her "Wino Uniform."

It snowed on Christmas Eve and we ordered in Chinese food. Pete's older brother and sister were there and it had been decided we would exchange presents that night, as I had agreed to a double shift at the nursing home and Pete's family would be driving up to

Massachusetts early Christmas morning to visit some ancient relatives. His father gave me a copy of Hunter S. Thompson's Fear and Loathing in Las Vegas. I presented him a gallon of pepper-infused vodka, which still a novelty in 1982. By 8 p.m., we were smashed. Pete's dad had passed out on the living room floor, in front of the tree. At his mother's urging, Pete and I stuck a bow on his dad's forehead and covered him up with the discarded wrapping paper. We giggled uncontrollably, as we ate chicken wings and watched The Christmas Carol on the television.

After an hour or so, Pete's dad began to stir beneath the tree. We could hear him groaning above the sound of rustling paper. Then he began to fart. They were fierce, angry farts. He sat up suddenly, red-faced and sweating, and pointed at me.

"Goddamn you, Jeffrey, get me some water! This peppered-vodka has set my asshole on fire!"

I went to the kitchen to get him a glass of water. When I returned, he had stripped down to his boxer shorts and was hopping in place, as if dancing on hot coals.

"It fucking hurts. It really hurts."

His wife and children were laughing hysterically.

"It's not funny!"

Pete's dad pulled off his shorts and ran outside into the snow. We all moved to the window. He was laying on his back in the front yard, naked in the snow. Pete's mom went to the door.

"Get inside, you jackass! You'll get arrested if the neighbors see you," she yelled.

"Fuck you! I'm the ghost of Christmas future. I'm

the ghost of Christmas future!"

He began to flap his arms and legs, sweeping them across the ground.

"He's making a snow angel," said Pete.

We looked to each other and smiled. We stripped off our clothes and ran out to join his father in the snow. We giggled uncontrollably—three naked men, laying side-by-side, making snow angels.

JELLYFISH

Ramona's earliest memory is of the jellyfish. It was her eighth birthday and her father had driven their family down to Atlantic City in his pearl-white Buick. He was a stout little man with stubby fingers and hair the color of coal. He sold orthopedic supplies out of an office he had converted from the garage of their Flatbush home. Ramona's mother was a sickly woman who chain-smoked Pall Malls and regardless of the season, was rarely seen in public without the ratty fox stole that had once belonged to her mother. The three and a half hour drive to the Tropicana had been miserable due to beach traffic and her father's insistence that they would save on gas if they didn't run the air conditioning.

Once they reached the hotel, her parents deposited Ramona and her two-year old sister, Larissa, on the beach and hurried to the casino. They didn't seem to notice that the beach was closed. It was a humid June afternoon and there was not even the slightest breeze in the air. Red warning flags hung lifelessly from their poles as the lifeguards sat bored and motionless in their towers, their tanned skin damp with perspiration. The hot sand scorched her feet as Ramona led her sister down to the water—she thought the ground would be cooler there. It was then that she saw the massive bloom of jellyfish and understood why the beach had been closed. There were hundreds of them floating in the ocean, their pink flesh billowing in the tide as they slowly crept to shore. A wave crashed on the beach, stranding several of the jellyfish on the sand—their thread-like tentacles baking in the sun as they slowly suffocated.

Ramona wanted to help but was afraid to touch them. She was relieved to see another wave strike the beach, the retreating tide dragging a few of the jellyfish back out to sea. She wondered whether it was God that decided which ones would be left behind or if it was simply chance. She wondered whether jellyfish had families. Ramona watched them for hours, as her sister built cities in the sand and her mother wandered the slot machines with her oxygen tank and a gin and tonic. The two sisters caught nasty sunburns that day, their skin had turned beet red by the time mother came to collect them from the beach. They spent the evening in the hotel room, shaking with fever as their mother fed them salt-water taffy and ginger ale.

For her tenth birthday, Ramona's father showed her his penis. She woke up that night to find him sitting in a chair at the foot of her bed. The room was dark but the embers from his cigarette cast just enough light to make out the contours of his chubby frame beneath a tattered, flannel robe.

"Daddy?"

He said nothing. Instead, he parted the folds of his robe, revealing his erection. He leaned back in his chair and blew smoke rings at her as he wrapped his stubby little fingers around his dick and began to masturbate. She rolled over on her side, turning her back to him. She shut her eyes, pretending to be asleep. Still, she could hear him—his labored breathing and the clumsy sound of pawing flesh.

Ramona's father repeated this ritual for several nights, each evening moving his chair a little closer to her bedside. Eventually, he began to touch her, gently at first but before long so roughly, she could no longer pretend to be asleep. Eventually, he made her touch him. Ramona can't remember when he started fucking her. But she would never forget the weight of his body on top of her and the slightly pungent taste of his sweat. Ramona's mother never seemed to notice that her bedroom always smelled of cigarettes.

By the time Ramona was twelve, he was raping her twice a day. No longer content to visit her in her room at night, Ramona's father would call her into his office every afternoon when she returned from school. It was a cold, damp space that was filled with orthopedic supplies. He rarely said a word when she entered. Rather, he would just bend her over a box of artificial hips, and fuck her from behind. He always placed his hand over her mouth, to insure Ramona's mother—who was now bed-ridden with emphysema—would not hear them. His hands always smelled of whatever he had eaten for lunch that day and Ramona found the scents overwhelming. She invented a game in which she would close her eyes and try to recreate the shapes of the porcelain bones that surrounded her. She found it distracted her from the smells of tuna fish salad and hard-boiled eggs.

At age thirteen, Ramona began to grow. Indeed, she grew to be unusually tall for her age, with broad shoulders and wide hips. This was frustrating to Ramona's father because he found he could no longer wrap his stubby fingers around her waist when raping her. It was then that he decided to install the handles. The operation took place late at night, on the workbench in his garage. He had fashioned two porcelain handles, which after sedating her with a combination of Seconal and Bailey's Irish Cream, he attached to her hips using long, stainless steel screws. She awoke several hours later in great pain. Her father had returned her to her bed, tying her arms to the bedposts so she could not reach her newly installed accessories. Ramona was surprised to find him there beside her, asleep in his chair.

Over the next several weeks, Ramona's father tended to her every need. She remembers this time period as a happy one, mostly because he had stopped raping her. And although she was restrained, she was rarely bored. Her father had bought her a small color television, which he placed at the foot of her bed. By day, she watched soap operas while he fed her soup. At night he read her Nancy Drew mystery stories. He had never read to her before. Ramona's father cleaned her wounds religiously, taking great care to insure that they healed quickly and with only minimal scarring. One night, having taken a bottle of her mother's nail polish, he painted a single red rose on each of Ramona's porcelain handles. Ramona's wounds were fully healed by the end of the summer, so her father began raping her once again. Her handles were the perfect size for his chubby little fingers, enabling him a firm grip on her hips when he fucked her.

On Labor Day weekend, Ramona learned that she would not be returning to school that year. Her father had decided that she would be home-schooled but she never opened another textbook again. Instead, he took her on the road with him. They visited hospitals across upstate New York, the backseat of their car filled with artificial knees and prosthetic limbs. At night they stayed in motor inns, where the sheets irritated her skin and smelled vaguely of fast food and semen. Late at night, Ramona would lay in bed with her father asleep beside her—always with a fat little hand gripping one of her hips. The walls were so thin she could hear couples fucking in the neighboring rooms. She wondered what the women looked like and what they were doing that made them cry out so happily and sometimes, even laugh. She wondered if any of them had handles too.

Ramona's father raped her across Schenectady, Rochester, and Buffalo. Sometimes he let her drive the old, white Buick. About twice a month, they would return home for a day or two. Her father would get his suits pressed and Ramona would play with her sister on the rusty swing set in the backyard. Sometimes, if her mother was feeling up to it, Ramona would sit with her in her bedroom and play gin rummy. Her mother rarely left her room at all anymore.

When Ramona was fourteen, she got her first period. A few days later, her father abandoned her outside of Niagara Falls. It happened so easily. He pulled into a gas station and sent Ramona in to buy him cigarettes. When she came out of the store, he was gone. Ramona was left with nothing but thirteen dollars and a pack of Winstons. She sat on the curb for several hours, until a trucker offered her a ride. He tried to rape her in Scranton, Pennsylvania but threw her out of the cab once he saw her porcelain handles. Over the next several months,

Ramona learned that most men did not enjoy her enhancements. She traveled across the country, trading rides and meals for blowjobs. At least then, she didn't have to take off her clothes.

Ramona was sixteen when she met Magic Mike at a Waffle House in West Virginia. He worked at a body-piercing studio in Morgantown. His arms were covered in tattoos and he wore a silver ring in his nose. Ramona thought he was the most beautiful boy she had ever seen. Magic Mike took her on his motorcycle to a nearby lake, where they fed crusts of bread to the ducks. He told her funny stories that made her laugh so hard she snorted and when he kissed her, it was as soft and sweet as a baby's kiss. Ramona loved him instantly.

Later that night, when he undressed her and saw the porcelain handles, he was not repulsed but fascinated. And when she explained their origin and how she came to be in West Virginia, he did not pity her. He just smiled and took off his clothes, leaving Ramona breathless. She was surprised to find that virtually his entire body was covered in tattoos, an endless landscape of shipwrecks, skeletons, and pin-up girls. They did not have sex that night. Rather, they spent the evening surveying his flesh, Ramona trailing a finger along every line of ink, drinking in the color and warmth of his skin as he narrated the story of each tattoo. They were inseparable after that, Ramona and Magic Mike. And while they occasionally argued, they stayed mostly in love.

It was Mike who suggested they cut off the porcelain handles. It had never occurred to Ramona that they could be removed. Although bone tissue had long since grown over the screws at the point where they joined her hips, Magic Mike suggested they saw off the head of the screws at the surface of the skin, where something that was more to Ramona's liking could be attached. He spent the next several days sketching different designs for Ramona's approval. He was partial to garnet studs.

It was Ramona who first thought of the thorns. Forged in surgical steel and molded in the shape of a rose thorn, each implant would be attached to the screw stems that protruded from Ramona's hips. Mike quickly located a foundry to cast the thorns. The procedure was relatively painless and created the illusion that two metal thorns had sprouted from Ramona's hips. When the operation was over, Ramona placed the porcelain handles in an old cigar box that Mike kept coins in. Although they made sex a little awkward, the thorns excited Magic Mike. He liked to imagine he was fucking an alien, like that monster from the Predator movies. Ramona had never been happier. She was glad to be rid of the handles and the thorns made her feel beautiful and dangerous.

It wasn't long before Ramona wanted more. So Magic Mike redesigned the thorns as transdermal implants. Before long, Ramona was covered in thorns. A row of them trailed down her spine, while others adorned her forearms and thighs. Ramona grew lovelier with each new thorn. Her eyes turned a brighter shade of blue and her skin as smooth and white as the porcelain handles that had once scarred her.

By the time she was seventeen, Ramona had become something of a local celebrity and began modeling for alternative magazines and pin-up calendars. Magic Mike was her tireless promoter, constantly updating her Facebook page and booking her on modeling gigs. At eighteen, she landed the cover of Bizarre magazine and they moved to Los Angeles. Ramona loved that the sun was always shining there and how the beaches stretched on for miles.

Later that year, Ramona and Magic Mike traveled to Brooklyn for the annual Mermaid Parade. He had booked Ramona for an appearance at the Coney Island Circus Sideshow. Ramona felt very much at home with the snake charmers, sword-swallowers, and bearded ladies. She performed an exotic dance in which she emerged from a small wooden box, like a rose bush sprouting up from the soil. The audience, comprised mostly of punks and hipsters, adored her.

She had barely recognized Larissa, standing in the crowd. She no longer had the face of an eight year-old but of a prepubescent girl. Larissa had long gangly arms and an awkward face that was marred with acne. Their eyes met in a flash of recognition and shared anguish that was instantly familiar to Ramona. They went for a hot dog after the show. Ramona's mom had died two years earlier, finally succumbing to emphysema. Ramona didn't have to ask whether her father was raping Larissa.

Later that evening, Ramona quietly entered the Flatbush house, surprised to find that her key still worked. She tiptoed up the stairs and into Larissa's room, only to find her alone and sleeping soundly. She moved down the hall to what had once been her mother's bedroom. Her father had covered all the furniture with sheets, except for the oxygen tank, which stood in the corner of the room—the only evidence that Ramona's mother had ever existed.

She slowly crept down the stairs and into her father's office. Ramona found him at his desk, half-asleep and surrounded with empty beer cans and orthopedic supplies. He was wearing his familiar flannel robe and his hair, now long and unkempt, had turned grey. His eyes grew wide when he saw her, as if she were an apparition.

"Have you come back to me?"

Ramona nodded as she began to undress. Her father flashed a greasy smile as he opened his tattered robe and began to touch himself. But as Ramona slipped out of her dress, revealing her suit of thorns, his expression changed to one of horror.

"What have you done with my handles?" he asked.

Ramona picked up a titanium femur from his desk and smashed it over his head. Later, when he regained consciousness, he found she had strapped him to his workbench. She stood over him, grinning, the two porcelain handles in her palm.

"I've saved these for you," she said.

Ramona attached the rose-covered handles to her father's head, using a power drill and stainless steel screws. She muffled his screams with the folds of his bathrobe but he only lasted a few minutes before blacking out.

"You've grown so fat," she muttered to herself. "How will I ever carry you?"

Looking around, Ramona quickly found a solution. His head came off easily with a surgical saw.

In June of her eighteenth year, Ramona drove down to Atlantic City in her father's pearl-white Buick, his head resting on the passenger seat beside her. It was nearly 5 am by the time she reached the Tropicana. The boardwalk was deserted this time of night. There was no one to notice her as she walked out to the beach, carrying her father's head, her long fingers gripped around a rose-covered handle. She was surprised how heavy it was.

When she reached the water's edge, Ramona tossed her father's head into the ocean. It bobbed in the tide for a few minutes, his long grey hair expanding like tentacles in the water. Ramona watched the head as it was slowly pulled out to sea. She sat on the beach as the sun came up, wondering if she would see any jellyfish.

THERE IS A MOTEL ROOM IN MY HEAD

There is a motel room in my head
where the bed is never made
and you always arrive with candles
and a red bulb for the lamp,
where the clothes ripped from your body
lie in ruins of torn silk
on carpets soaked in wine and ash.

There is a motel room in my head
where I wash your hair
and kiss painted toes
one by one,
and soapy fingers find hidden roses
crowned in silver in gardens of flesh and ink
freshly scalded from the tub.

There is a motel room in my head
where there is no place for regret
and words fail miserably
to capture the bluebird's song,
found in the cadence of your breath
and every heartbeat counted
as you sleep with warm hand on cock.

There is a motel room in my head
where I drink from your cunt
as fingers tighten around your throat

and we fuck until there is love instead of despair,
and plaster walls dissolve into a sea of stars
and our bed is but a gutter
of tears, sweat and come.

There is a motel room in my head
where the light is always on.

UNSPOKEN (FOR SIREN)

Nestled in my lap, your knees tucked beneath you
in a worn shirt that smells of me.
Me, drowning in you.

There is a hint of thigh there and creamy white leg,
marred with the imprint of rough hands
and fingers still slick with excitement.

You read me a story, as we share a cigarette
and a jelly jar filled with whisky.
My fingers keep rhythm with the lilt and meter of your
voice,
as they run through your hair and the peaks and valleys,
that hide in the glorious space between your neck and
shoulders.

I close my eyes, so as to let your voice carry me away.
It is a voice so sweet it could be mistaken for that of a
child,
if only it did not speak of murder and loss,
and the sorrow of old bones turned to dust.
It is the voice of the orphan, the hustler, the hooker and
the pimp.
A voice filled with vinegar and spit,
and the laughter of drunks who find humor and life,
in the cracks between everything.

It is a voice that is hundreds of years old and so familiar,
that it finds me in all of the places in which l hide.
I could listen to this voice forever.

TREEHOUSE

gretchen gretchen gretchen
the name hung on his tongue
like sugar cubes and rye
it was a rich girl's name
a connecticut name
a girl who smelled of flowers
and whose bra matched her panty
that matched her nails
yeah girls named gretchen
had it all figured out

but not her
she wasn't rich
she didn't have it
figured out
but when she opened her mouth
she was fearless
she had conviction
plain-spoken
midwestern
honesty

and when he peeled off her underwear
her hair was as bright and orange
as the sun
pulling him in like a lost astronaut
like fruit flies to whiskey

with legs so long and beautiful
when wrapped around him
he dreamed of treehouses
swaying in the breeze
tall enough to touch the stars

GINNY'S BIG NIGHT

Ginny didn't care much for Uncle Robby and had purposely not invited him to the wedding. This was largely due to the fact that his breath always smelled like onions and coffee, and he had once "accidentally" brushed his hand against her breast when she was fourteen—not to mention the bathrobe incident. Ginny stopped having sleepovers with her cousin Ruthie after that. Still, Robby was her uncle and she could not refuse her mother when she insisted that Ginny extend him an invitation.

She sat Uncle Robby at the "singles' table." He got drunk on Jack and Cokes and ate two plates of prime rib, all the while sitting uncomfortably close to Ginny's childhood friend, Jeanine Russo. Ginny knew she shouldn't let Uncle Robby distract her from this special day but she felt her face grow flush with anger as she watched him shadow her girlfriends onto the dance floor, injecting himself into every Hustle, his unwelcome hands wrapping around their waists as he awkwardly swung his hips in their direction, straining to make contact with anything that was warm and soft. Uncle Robby was not the least bit deterred by their forced smiles and polite redirection of his hands. Of course, Ginny's husband, Chris, was oblivious to Robby's behavior, which annoyed her but it was also one of the reasons she loved him so much. He was a gentle soul and tended to look for the good in everyone. Ginny often teased him that he "could find a rainbow in a stream of piss." He just sat quietly beside her at the bridal table, occasionally stroking her hand as he sipped his O'Doul's with a goofy smile.

The next two hours passed uneventfully, until Uncle Robby began to clang a fork against his wine glass. Having captured the attention of the banquet hall, he rose unsteadily to his feet and stumbled across the room to the bridal table. He positioned himself between Ginny and Chris, and raised a near-empty glass into the air as he placed his other arm around Ginny's shoulder. He was drenched in sweat, which smelled of whiskey and that stale, familiar odor of cigarettes and onions. Ginny gagged slightly as he offered a toast.

"Doesn't Ginny look beautiful tonight? Ain't they beautiful kids?"

Ginny looked to Chris nervously, as the guests responded with polite, measured applause.

"I watched Ginny grow up with my little Ruthie," Robby slurred. "I think she's here tonight."

His voice trailed off into an extended and uncomfortable silence. Ginny spotted Ruthie seated at a table near the door. Embarrassed, Ruthie avoided Ginny's gaze. Uncle Robby drained his glass of the last sip of Jack and Coke.

"Enjoy each other. Enjoy your youth. You know, you never forget being young," he said with a smile as his hand fell off Ginny's shoulder and snaked down to the small of her back.

"When you're young, everything tastes different…everything smells better."

Ginny stiffened as she politely inched away from him.

"These days, everything I put in my mouth is salt,"

said Uncle Robby, a hint of bitterness in his voice.

Ginny's mother signaled to the D.J. as she quickly moved to the table and grabbed Robby by the arm. K.C. and the Sunshine Band filled the room as Ginny's mother escorted Robby to the bar. Chris shrugged his shoulders at Ginny.

"I guess your uncle had too much to drink," he offered with a dopey smile, completely unaware of what had transpired.

Furious, Ginny excused herself and walked quickly to the restroom. It was there that she found Ruthie crying. It was then that she learned that Uncle Robby used to open his robe and make Ruthie sit on his lap while he watched the Honeymooners and laughed at the television set.

Later, Ginny emptied a small bottle of Visine into Uncle Robby's ninth glass of Jack and Coke. He became violently ill and shit his pants. He vomited several times before he was taken to the emergency room. For years, Ginny's mom would be heard to complain that Uncle Robby had spoiled the wedding but Ginny looks back fondly on the memory of her uncle being carried from the reception hall on a stretcher, diarrhea running down his pant leg. Chris was the only one who noticed that Ginny was giggling as the ambulance drove away.

Back in their hotel room, Ginny finally told Chris all about Uncle Robby and confessed to poisoning him at the reception. While Chris was stunned, he had to concede that he felt a little turned on by what Ginny had done. In his mind, their marriage had been ordained with an egregious sin against God and man, and it was a secret they would forever share. For her part, poisoning Uncle Robby made Ginny feel like a badass. It made her feel sexy. She would never tell Chris but she always believed that the sex they had on their wedding night was the best she ever had.

THE WIG

From the moment she first saw the old hatbox, Elizabeth felt drawn to it. She found it in the back of her mother's closet, sitting on a shelf above Aunt Dot's wedding dress. Elizabeth was only eight when Dottie committed suicide, just two weeks before her wedding day and under circumstances that had never been fully explained to Elizabeth. Her mother had rarely spoken of her aunt and Elizabeth never imagined that she would have kept the gown. But seeing it there, with Dot's name written hastily on a faded receipt stapled to the garment bag, Elizabeth realizes that the dress must have served as a protective totem, warning all those that entered the closet to stay away. Certainly, her father would not have ventured any further after seeing the dress and knowing the significance attached to it.

Her father had always avoided any activity that might result in confrontation or elicit strong emotions. Every step he took, every word he uttered, seemed carefully calibrated. Elizabeth cannot remember a single instance in which he so much as raised his voice. Before retiring last year, he had spent 30 years as a postman. She wonders if he ever missed a day of work. She liked to imagine him delivering the mail. Of course, he would take the same route every day, taking slow, deliberate steps under a hot sun. He would stop occasionally to notice a flower in bloom or to make small talk with Mrs. Nelson, who could always be found waiting anxiously at her mailbox for a letter that never came. Sometimes she invites him inside for a cold drink but he always politely declines.

Sometimes, after a third vodka gimlet, her mother would taunt him from across the dinner table.

"Your father is so slow, Elizabeth. Slow and steady, and painfully dull."

She liked to ride him in front of Elizabeth, to talk about him as if he weren't even there. He never responded. He never challenged her. Instead, he just stared grimly into his peas. His passivity only made her angrier. She would push her plate away in disgust, then storm off to the porch for a Pall Mall. Only then, would he look up from his plate and offer Elizabeth a reassuring smile.

"Sometimes it's better to be kind than to be right."

She never understood what he meant by that. Nor did she understand her mother's periodic flashes of mean-spiritedness. Now, as she pulls the box down from the shelf and places it on the bed, she realizes she never will.

It's been two weeks since the cancer took her, here in this room. In the end, she wanted to be at home. Elizabeth and her father sat vigil beside her, watching soap operas, changing her oxygen tanks, and waiting for her to die. It happened during a game of gin rummy. She slipped away so quietly they didn't realize she had gone. There was no last gasp, no final words—just a clenched fist with three queens never discarded.

Elizabeth stares intently at the hatbox on the bed. Already, it has lent an air of mystery to the room, which at her father's request, she has scrubbed clean of any traces of her mother. It has taken Elizabeth all day to pack up her mother's belongings. Her husband, Paul, drove her up to Connecticut from their home on Long Island. It was a pleasant ride, mostly because the leaves were changing to red and gold, and other than the incessant chatter of the AM radio, the trip was made in silence. Paul was a tireless consumer of news. At home, he always had the television set on CNN. He would listen intently to the same stories as they cycled over and over again, as if waiting for something to happen. It used to bother her but now she has grown accustomed to the noise. It is as much a part of her environment as the small talk she shares with her husband.

"How was your day?"
"This is a nice wine."
"It looks like snow."
Lifeless words that go largely unacknowledged, like the fly on a horse's mane.

Elizabeth can't remember when they stopped having conversations.   Sometimes it seems as if they've just run out of things to share. She knows she should feel some sadness or resentment, but she doesn't. Paul is a good and patient man. Together, they packed up her mother's shoes and clothing, an assortment of picture frames, and an extensive collection of knitting magazines that spanned nearly fifty years. Her life fit neatly into a dozen boxes, which Paul dutifully carried up to the attic before retreating to the den to watch football with her father. Nothing remains but the hatbox. It is decorated in a simple floral pattern. Flowering vines of wisteria stretch across a pearl white background. The paper has turned yellow in places, its edges cracked and frayed. The words "Marshall Field's" are printed on the lid in a beautiful cursive font. Beneath it, appears "Chicago, U.S.A.," in bold letters. Elizabeth smiles. When she was young, her mother would go to Chicago for knitting conventions. She often took such trips, sometimes two or three times a year.

Elizabeth opens the box. Inside sits a wig of long chestnut hair. She frowns. Her mother never wore hairpieces. Until the cancer came, she had thick, blond curls. Elizabeth holds it up to the light. The netting is torn in places from wear. She notices a stack of letters inside the box, bundled together with a piece of ribbon. She pulls an envelope from the stack and opens it. Three photographs fall to the floor. That's when all the air goes out and Elizabeth drops to her knees.

The first photograph she sees is of her mother and another woman. They are both naked from the waist up. Her mother is wearing the wig and one of her arms is draped around the neck of the other woman. They are laughing. The second photograph is of her mother on a bed. Again, she is naked. She is on her hands and knees as the headless torso of a man fucks her from behind. Her expression is wanton. It is a look Elizabeth has never seen on her mother's face. She wonders who took the photograph.

It is several minutes before Elizabeth can bring herself to look at the third photograph, which depicts her mother and a group of friends at a restaurant. Her mother is wearing the wig. The men are dressed in suits, while the women wear fancy cocktail dresses. Never in her life has Elizabeth seen her mother in such a dress. She holds a martini glass in her hand. Elizabeth's face turns flush with anger. Who are these people? Who is this woman with the long, chestnut hair?

Elizabeth spends the next two hours examining each photograph and letter in the hatbox, a secret history of love affairs and sex parties stretching across the United States. By her count, there are more than thirty photographs. Her mother, wearing the wig, is depicted in nearly all of them; giving a blowjob in St. Louis or at an orgy in Tahoe, or with her face nestled between a woman's thighs in San Diego. While some letters hint at casual friendships and anonymous sex, other reveal her mother's deep, intimate friendships with people Elizabeth has never even heard of. And although she feels a little sickened at the sight of her mother having sex, the photographs fascinate her. The acts depicted are not all that different than the sexual fantasies Elizabeth has secretly enjoyed for years.

She picks up the wig and slips it onto her head. She looks into the mirror and wonders what her mother felt like the first time she put it on. It is then that Elizabeth notices she is crying. She wonders if she is angry over her mother's betrayal or grieving for the loss of a stranger.

"Libby?" calls her husband from the stairs

She quickly removes the wig from her head and returns it to the hatbox, along with her mother's letters and photographs. When Paul opens the door, Elizabeth is sitting on the bed with the hatbox on her lap.

"You okay?" he asks. "You've been in here for hours."

She nods half-heartedly.

"We should hit the road before it gets dark."

He gestures to the hatbox.

"Do you want me to put that up in the attic for you?"

"No," says Elizabeth. "I'd like to bring this home."

THE LOVERS

"Let's make love," he says, knowing how much it irritates her.

She grimaces.

"Can't we just fuck instead?"

Their sex is never beautiful. There is no sweet caress, no tenderness or purr. She does not seduce him, rather she screams at him with her cunt. She will stare him down with glorious demanding tits, until he succumbs to a hard fuck on the bathroom floor.

Their bodies are too needy for romance. They have abandoned soft sheets and butterfly kisses for angry fucks in parked cars and a blowjobs in bathroom stalls. Their sex is gnashing and tearing, with foul-mouth and salted tears.

Their lust is greedy and crude. He thinks nothing of slipping a hand inside her shirt when standing in line at the supermarket. She smiles at the cashier while she rubs his cock through his jeans.

Their sex is never beautiful. It is purple bruises and dirty feet.

WHAT WE LEARN FROM MONARCHS

He did not fall in love when he fucked her in the stairwell
with dirty knees and hands clutched tightly around throat.

And she shed no tears for the ghosts he carried in his
pocket
with money for whores and unfinished poems.
Her tears were hers alone.

But beneath summer's open window, a butterfly flew in
and settled with broken wing upon her thigh.

For nine days it lived with them in their bed,
surviving on sugar water and fluttering from knee to
breast
as she came with lips pressed against her cunt.

And on the tenth day, its wings stopped beating.
It was only then that she wept and his heart exploded.

SAINT HANK

We lie in bed at 3 am.
It's never clear how we got there.
We come from a different place and time,
shedding dampened clothes like skin,
and hours of the day and memories
unwanted as unclean fingers
in cunt and mouth.

We lie dirty with sweat and spit,
naked and panting beneath dripping candles,
and scraps of paper and flesh.
etched with heated words of lovers.
It is your breath that makes my cock reach
like broken sailors long for stars
and jagged shores.

You read to me aloud.
It is Bluebird, a Bukowski poem.
It has been years since I've heard it spoken,
my own tongue having mangled it
with acid and regret,
I wrote him off as another drunk
who beat his wife.

But from your lips,
his words carry a strength
and desire that makes my heart float

like a Byron poem or hot air balloon,
descending upon our bed to feast,
on spreading legs and whispers
that poet never knew.

CONTEMPLATION

Del Withers sits in a tub half-filled with water, quietly shaving her legs as she considers the best way to get rid of her children. By "best way" she does not mean the most effective way but simply the method that will cause her the least amount of grief while still insuring that no one will ever find out. Del leans back into the luke-warm water and blows a damp ringlet of blonde hair from her eyes. She's pretty sure that killing your children would be thought of as a horrible deed in anybody's book—one of those things people hear about on the evening news that causes them to shake their heads and wonder what on earth could ever cause someone to commit such an act against a child. Still, she hasn't made up her mind yet. Is it a sin just to contemplate the act? Del is pretty sure it is, at least that's what Maddy would say if she were still alive.

She wonders whether "contemplating" is a nicer word than "planning." She likes the word contemplating. It was the first word she saw after she hung up with Glen, just glaring at her from Maddy's 2004 Word of the Day calendar. Of course, it wasn't 2004 and hadn't been for some time; not since Maddy Withers had died and Del had never bothered to throw away the calendar. In fact, she had paid little notice to that calendar until the morning Glen called, just 2 days ago.

"I'm out of here in 5 days, sugar. I want to see that pretty smile when I walk through those gates."

Glen spoke in a tone that was simultaneously sweet and threatening; so much so that it made the soft little hairs on the back of Del's neck stand up. That was when the planning or better said, the contemplating, began.

Del knows she can make the drive to Huntsville in about three days. That's how long it had taken her to drive up from the prison to Maddy's house in upstate New York thirteen years ago. She had felt guilty about leaving Glen as he had no real family to speak of, but she couldn't shake the nagging feeling that the relationship had run its course. There was nothing to bind her to Texas except for Glen and he would be spending the next fifteen years in an eight by six box, leaving her nothing but a near-empty efficiency apartment in La Porte, for which she was more than 2 months behind on the rent. Any savings they had at the time he was arrested, which wasn't much because Glen's temper had rendered him largely unemployable during their time in Texas, had gone to the lawyers. Del still had her job at Dow Chemical then but it was only minimum wage and she had no real friends to speak of there. Upon her hiring, she had found that she was widely resented for being too young, too pretty, or too white.

Their farewell had been strained and awkward. Glen tried to maintain his pride, telling her over and over that he would be okay and that it was best for her to go back to Yorktown, where at least, she had family. Still he could not resist demanding that she stay faithful, and that she call and write at least once a week. Of course, Del had promised she would, even though at the time, she had no intention of doing so. All she had wanted was to get as far away from Glen and La Porte as she possibly could.

And so she ran. Back home to Aunt Maddy's tired old Victorian in Yorktown. She had been just 15 when she left for Texas, having known Glen for only a few days. It took a year or so for everything to fall apart, to be penniless and miserable and at each other's throats all the time, and for Glen to kill a man without really meaning to.

To her credit, Maddy never said "I told you so," although Del knew she must have been thinking it the morning she pulled into her aunt's driveway in Glen's pickup. Maddy just walked down from the porch and gave Del a long, sincere hug, shrugged her shoulders, and helped her carry her things up to her room. Maddy never expressed disappointment in anyone; frequent failures were to be expected, if not anticipated, in the Withers family. Even when Del announced that she was pregnant, less than two months after her return to Yorktown, Maddy expressed no disappointment or shame. If anything, she was excited at the thought of having a young child around the house again.

The water is turning cool and goose bumps rise on Del's breasts and forearms. She steps out of the tub, taking a moment to admire her figure in the bathroom mirror. Del had kept her form, despite having given birth to twins—everyone said so. She smiles slyly, guessing Glen would think the same. Of course, Glen didn't know about the twins. He could never know.

The twins came earlier than expected, just eleven

months after Del arrived unceremoniously in Yorktown and nearly two years since the last time she had been intimate with Glen. Not that they had ever been truly "expected." Rather, the twins had been the final salvo in a series of sudden, unexpected events, which began with the surprise appearance of Ginny Russo's Toyota Celica in her aunt's driveway, just two nights after Del's return to Yorktown. Prior to her leaving for Texas with Glen, Ginny and Del had been best friends, inseparable partners in crime who had ruled Yorktown High School with a ruthlessness and lack of foresight that was typical of popular teenage girls. Prior to her arrival in Maddy's driveway, they had not seen each other in over a year. But there she was, leaning on the horn with a Salem 100 stuck between her fingers and the Red Hot Chile Peppers blaring from her car stereo. Ginny just hooted and screamed, "Del Withers, get your butt down here. We're gonna find us some pretty long-haired boys tonight," in her distinctly smoky but feminine voice. And Del, who had been sulking for two days on Maddy's living room couch alternating between fits of self-pity and anger at Glen, was only too happy to oblige.

The sun is starting to go down and a cool breeze blows in through the bathroom window. Del wonders whether it will rain tonight as she wraps a towel around herself and thinks of Ginny Russo, singing "Give it Away" at the top of her lungs as they sped down the Taconic Parkway toward New York City with a bottle of Southern Comfort stolen from Mr. Russo's liquor cabinet.

Even now, Del can remember the wind in her hair and the slow burn of the Comfort on her throat. She had nearly finished the bottle by the time they reached the city and was fixing to get even with Glen for shooting a man and getting himself and darn near Del arrested in the process. They hopped from bar to bar until they had landed in a dirty little shithole in the East Village called "Downtown Beirut." Ginny had thought it sounded exotic. The crowd had been an uneasy mix of punk rockers, metal heads, and old men that smelled like cigarettes and pee but in the midst of it all shined the prettiest boy Del had ever seen. His name was Marcus and he had long, ash-white hair and eyes that were so green they made Del think of the Bahamas travel brochures that Maddy displayed, without explanation, on her coffee table. (Maddy had only taken but one trip in her entire life, to the Smithsonian Institution in Washington D.C.) Marcus had a beautiful mouth, with soft, pink lips that made Del think of movie star kisses. Del had wanted him from the moment she saw him; to get carried away in a tangle of his long blond hair. They hadn't had but a couple of shots before Del took him by the hand and led him to the backseat of Ginny's Celica. And Marcus had been everything those lips had advertised and nothing at all like Glen. He was sweet, pretty, and quietly self-assured. And after he was gone, Del laughed. She laughed until she started to cry, and then cried until she threw up. Del never drank Southern Comfort again.

Her series of unexpected events continued when two months later, she discovered she was pregnant. She was even more surprised to learn that she was carrying twins, the undoubtedly fair-haired and pretty children of Marcus, a man whose last name she had never bothered to ask and who she did not expect to ever see again. Still, as much as Del wanted to get an abortion, she just couldn't bring herself to do it. Del's dad had taken off before she was born and her mom not much longer after that. Save for Maddy, she had no one. To Del, it seemed her universe was just getting smaller and smaller. It wasn't too hard to conclude that having those babies wasn't such a bad idea. At least it would stop her world from shrinking.

It didn't. Del dropped out of Yorktown High after she began to show. Ginny started coming by less and less, until it seemed as if they were no longer friends. Occasionally, she would run into Ginny at the Seven-Eleven or at the bar where Del worked. Ginny would smile and make polite inquiries about her condition, and lament the fact that they never had time to speak anymore. She eventually went off to college. Del later learned she married a man from Kentucky and lives in a five thousand square foot house. Del couldn't imagine what she did with all that space. So it seemed for the longest time, there was only Del—who felt fat, tired, and miserable, and Maddy. Then the first of Glen's letters arrived.

Del felt nothing but dread the first time she opened the mailbox and found a letter addressed from Glen. At the time, it had been more than a year since she left Huntsville and had never written to him. She expected the letter to return all of the anger and disappointment she had felt toward Glen but it did not. Instead, it read:

Dear Delores,
I know I'm the last person you want to hear from but I just wanted to say that I'm sorry for making such a big mess of things

and for letting you down. Despite all the trouble we had, there were some good times too and I sure miss those. Hope life is treating you well.

Glen

In Del's experience, Glen had never been good with words. He just tended to do what needed to be done and if he spoke at all, it was just to express, often forcefully and in as few words as possible, some practical need or the current state of affairs.

"I'm hungry."

"I'm horny."

"I'm tired."

"I shot him dead."

While Glen's letter had made it clear he was no Shakespeare, it still made her cry. In Del's view, he had scored some points for sincerity and for sharing the loneliness Del had been feeling since she got pregnant.

A couple of weeks later, Del worked up the courage to send a short letter in response. After that, Glen's letters came once a week. Del began to look forward to them. They often described his life in prison but Glen never complained or showed weakness. Del respected him for that. He even asked about her job and Aunt Maddy. And while Del could never bring herself to tell Glen about Marcus and the twins, a bond began to grow between them. After about year had passed, Glen began to sign his letters, "Love, Glen" instead of just "Glen." And it wasn't long after that when their letters began to hint at the idea of a future together. Del even found herself turning down dates with other men. On January 12, 2000, Del drove down to Huntsville to visit Glen for his birthday. It felt wonderful and electrifying just to hold his hand.

That thrill, which Del has experienced only two or three times a year since her first visit to Glen, is one of the few pleasures she has. She's never been much of a mother and won't pretend otherwise. Del's never been particularly interested in the development of the twins. No, if there had been any pride in parenting or nurturing of the children, it came from Maddy, and she has been dead for nearly five years.

If Del is to be honest with herself and it seems to her that standing naked in front of the bathroom mirror is a good time to be truthful, she must admit that she feels mostly resentment toward the twins. She looks at them and sees twelve years of lost opportunity and loneliness. They are the consequence of her betrayal of Glen and a terrible mistake that he must never know about.

Del opens the medicine cabinet and removes a bottle of sleeping pills.

TREES OF HEAVEN

Wyatt no longer enjoyed the taste of tobacco but he lit another cigarette just the same. The warm smoke helped fight the chill that had descended on the valley. He continued along the path, closing the collar of his flannel around his neck as a damp breeze shook the giant Virginia pines. Perhaps it was the bitterness of aging but it seemed to Wyatt that the autumn months were growing longer and colder; endless weeks of decay with a promise of rebirth that never seemed to come.

He stopped at the top of the hill, where he had found the Parker girl, her broken body propped up against the base of an Ailanthus tree, her hair speckled with its radiant orange seeds. It was one of the police officers who told him that the name meant "tree of heaven."' Wyatt didn't believe in heaven but he supposed if such a place existed, Amie Parker would likely be there.

It was springtime when he came upon her and at first, he thought nothing of finding her sitting alone under the tree. She had always kept to herself and had a reputation in town for being prone to daydreams and laughing inappropriately at inside jokes no one else understood. But as he drew closer he saw that her dress was torn, revealing a pale white breast and her once bright blue eyes had turned lifeless and grey as they stared down on the Little Miami River. It felt like hours until the police arrived, during which Wyatt had to resist the urge to brush the ants off of her dirty bare feet. He couldn't help but stare at her bloody mouth, which the killer had molded into a grim smile.

No one knew who murdered Amie Parker. The police had questioned Wyatt, along with most of the men in town, and concluded it was the work of a transient. He told them she came into the liquor store once a week to buy a quart of Jack Daniels for her mama. He didn't tell them that he occasionally snuck her miniature bottles of whiskey or about the time he fingered her in the storage locker in exchange for some cigarettes. And he didn't tell them that when he was alone at night, he frequently fantasized about the color of her panties and the soft skin on the inside of her thighs. After all, he wasn't the one who killed her and there was no reason to place suspicion on himself.

Wyatt has walked this path every day since he found Amie Parker under the Ailanthus tree. He tells himself it is in hope of finding some overlooked clue: a piece of fabric or perhaps a muddy shoe print. But all he really wants is capture some remnants of her life—to breathe the same air that she once did, and to find joy and comfort in being alone.

DREAM CATCHER

Hattie pulled the shoebox from its hiding place beneath her bed and opened it. It was filled with bric-a-brac gathered from around the farm over the past several weeks: some twine and pole nails found in the barn, a few shards of brightly colored glass from the root cellar, and a length of rusted barbed wire she uncovered in the cow pasture. Hattie fashioned the discarded items into a dream catcher, in the hopes it would trap nightmares instead. She hung it over her door, before she went to bed.

Hattie did not wake at the sound of plodding footsteps in the hall, his boots clumsy from too much whisky. But her eyes opened when an anxious hand opened her bedroom door, and bits of glass and steel rattled against wooden frame. Hattie reached for pawpaw's pocket knife, which she had placed beneath her pillow before falling asleep.

Her mother's voice sounded from the upstairs' bedroom.

"Ray, honey, is that you?"

He quickly retreated from Hattie's room, the sound of his footsteps growing fainter as he walked down the hall and up the stairs.

Hattie loosened her grip on the knife as she drifted off to sleep.

THE WAR OF BATS AND PORCUPINE

Your scent moves across my pillow,
like the spider descends upon fly.
But you have never graced this bed,
your absence pokes me with regret,
untold fortunes like porcupine quills.

So I lay here in sweat and tangled sheets,
the imagined folds of your skin.
Even by day, I dream of your cunt
and nipples so sweet,
they lure the butterfly.

I will turn out your garden like a swarm of bats,
and reduce your hive to dust.
And gnaw at your fruit and tangled webs,
until your ruddy hair hangs from my teeth
like the flickering lamp of the firefly.

THE AUDACITY OF LOVE

You won't find love in the color of her hair,
or in shaven cunts and sailor tattoos.
Love is foist upon you
when the trajectory of your scars
align perfectly with hers,
fingers entwined
that reach for the stars.

You won't find love in a mixtape,
in shared idols or dog-eared books.
Love is foist upon you
by soft lips and the cadence of her voice
that leaves you hanging
on every word
and fills your head with dreams.

Love tears your gaze from the gutter
leaving you to wonder
if she's looking at the same sky as you.

SPARROW'S CONCERN

We sit in a cafe in the French Quarter. It's only 8 a.m. but already more than 90 degrees in the shade. A handful of patrons have gathered for breakfast. They sit motionless at their tables, contemplating steaming plates of beignets—the exertion needed to eat them seems just too great. I'm nauseous from last night's whiskey and the heavy smell of powdered sugar that hangs in the air.

"I never thought donuts could be so oppressive," I quip.

You are not impressed. We've been here nearly twenty minutes and it's clear I'm about to get dumped. You take a deep breath before launching into a litany of my flaws. Apparently, I'm a self-absorbed, immature, obsessive drunk with unhealthy porn habits who is paralyzed by unrealistic expectations and a fear of failure.

I'm also emotionally detached.

The critique is a familiar one but one I cannot dispute. I shrug my shoulders, conceding your victory, as you begin to recount all the ways in which you've tried to salvage things and all the opportunities you've given me to reform.

I fall away from the conversation, focusing instead on two sparrows that have flown into the cafe from the adjoining garden. They flutter about the room, hopping from table to table in search of food. They chirp incessantly, silenced only by the morsels of pastry offered to them by the diners. I can't help but smile, their cheerfulness is contagious.

"Are you even listening to me?"

"Not really."

I barely notice you as you leave. The pair of sparrows has landed on the table of a heavyset man with short, stubby fingers. His face—red and swollen from the heat, is buried in the Times-Picayune. They sing to him as they flit their wings, eyeing a muffin that sits on the table before him. He looks up suddenly, startled to find them at his table. He swats them away with his newspaper, knocking one of the sparrows to the ground. The action is so swift and violent that at first, I think I just imagined it. But there lays the fallen sparrow at my feet, his partner darting about the lifeless body, flapping her wings in anguish. There is no more cheer in her song, only distress. I can feel the red-faced man's eyes upon me and realize I am crying. He eyes me coolly for a moment, then returns to his newspaper, leaving me to the grieving sparrow.

WHISKY ALWAYS TASTES
BETTER ON T.V.

Amos closes his eyes as he raises the glass to his lips. He inhales deeply, letting the whiskey fumes fill his nostrils and lungs, savoring the slow burn in his throat and the charcoal residue. He tilts his head back and lets the bourbon wash over his lips and tongue, and for a moment there is nothing but heat and spice.

Amos doesn't really care for whiskey. He and his brother used to sip Everclear on the roof of the double-wide. Rather, Amos relishes that first sip because it takes him somewhere far away; to a place that's always quiet and warm—a place that isn't here. It makes him think of his mother and the way she would sit on the porch in the summer, making charcoal sketches on big sheets of heavy white paper. He would sit beside her on the steps, watching her as she drew. She always worked in silence and sometimes hours would pass with hardly a word uttered between them. The pictures were always the same—detailed sketches of the day's laundry, hanging on the line—a pair of jeans or one of Aunt Dot's frilly slips, drying in the sun.

"Why do you always draw clothes?" he would ask.

"Things are prettier in my head," she would say, her eyes fixed on the paper.

Amos never developed a hand for art but he could lose himself in that first sip of whiskey. Bourbon brought him to his mother's smoky, charcoal-stained fingers and the stillness of those summer days. Whiskey brought him silence but for the August breeze rustling the trees or the distant bark of a dog.

It never lasts though. When he opens his eyes, Hattie is still there, chewing on her pencil. Twenty years of marriage hasn't taught Amos much about love. He's learned plenty about hate though. He hates the way she plays word jumble at the dinner table, while a cigarette burns in the ashtray and her dinner grows cold, and how her shit always smells faintly of coconut. He hates how she warms her ice cold feet against his legs when she crawls into their bed and the feel of her dry, calloused fingers on his cock. And he can't stand the way she blathers at him while she's brushing her teeth and her long searching looks as he descends the basement stairs to work on his dioramas. But mostly, Amos just hates himself, for not having decency to tell Hattie how he feels or the courage to leave her.

Hattie slaps her hand against the table.
I got it!" she exclaims, her eyes still on the newspaper. "Serendipity!"
Amos reaches for the bottle of Old Grand Dad as he gets up from the table and walks to the basement door.

LEAVE YOUR MONEY ON THE DRESSER

Charlie doesn't want to talk about his day.

Charlie just wants a blowjob.

He wants to leave his money on the dresser and drink hotel whiskey while a beautiful woman plays with his balls. He wants to drown in warm soft lips and spit, and fingers that don't feel like old bones and cold leather. He wants to explode in a mouth that remembers how to hide its disappointment and feign laughter at his jokes. He wants to look into eyes that can pretend he's someone he's not.

She unrolls a condom over his cock and takes him in her mouth. She looks up at him, wearing doe eyes and strained enthusiasm, but to Charlie her eyes look dull, like tarnished mirrors found in rich people's homes. When he looks at her, he sees nothing but his own mediocrity.

"Would you mind closing your eyes?" he asks.

THE WAIT

It was the moment before she emerged from the
bathroom that he enjoyed most,
after the money had been counted
and she checked in with her driver,
the mini bar consulted
and closet doors opened wide,
following the application of lip gloss
and spermicidal lubricant.

It was then that his heart quickened and his cock began
to stir,
imagining the softness of her pubic hair
and the velvety folds of her skin,
the weight of their manufactured histories
and taste of salt on his tongue,
wondering if she would fuck him
while chewing that apple-scented gum.

GLITTER HANDS

I fell in love with the stripper's smile,
hastened by glitter like stardust
and drunk on the dew that pooled
in the small of her back.

I fell in love with the stripper's eyes,
which matched my desire by the dollar
but reserved their adoration for pit bulls
rescued from so many shelters.

I fell in love with the stripper's hand,
embracing a hundred cocks through soiled denim
and burning her name in my skin
with ink and cunty fingers.

I fell in love with the stripper's tongue,
hesitant but warm with whiskey
and words meant only for me
and penned by my hand.

And when that stripper broke my heart,
I felt only longing.
The deceit had only been mine.

I DON'T WANT TO HOLD YOUR HAND

I don't want to hold your hand
or dry your tears
with butterfly kisses.

I want to rewrite history with your cunt
and carve our names
on tender anxious thighs,
sticky with come and menstrual blood.

I don't want to brush your silken hair
with careless whispers
and the tired promises of boys.

I want to wrench your hair in my fingers,
to coil it around your neck
until all the air is gone
and you choke on cock and balls.

I want to bind your feet and wrists,
and pinch your nipples
until swollen and sore
your skin smacked pink under a callous hand.

I want to fill your cunt with a poison tongue,
and dirty—no—filthy words
until there is nothing left

but greedy smiles and flesh falling happily from bone.

I don't want to fix what's broken
or cover your scars
with clumsy unclean hands.

I want to rewrite history with your cunt,
obliterate us in spit
and the fury of freshly bitten lips
until everything old feels new again.

POEM FOR A RALEIGH PROSTITUTE

Your fingers are a divining rod
finding rivers lost to dust and ash,
and though your ragged heart still keeps time,
like mine it beats
uneasily
in perpetuity for a song
written for another long ago.

I'll gladly pay an extra hundred
if we can pretend I know the words.

I FOUND LOVE AT THE OOH LA LA

Her momma named her Meredith or Merry for short, in the hopes she would have a cheerful disposition. Merry was never all that cheerful but she put out for any man that paid her the slightest bit of attention, so at least someone was happy.

When she was sixteen, momma threw her out for being a slut but Merry never saw it that way. She likes men. She likes the way they smell and the roughness of their skin. Her daddy left home when she was eight. Merry has little memory of him, except for his enormous hands and the tiny tattoo of a broken heart that sat between the base of his thumb and forefinger. She never knew what it meant.

*   *   *   *

Johnny Fuck Off isn't his real name but everyone calls him that on account of it being his first response to most any question.
"Hey, Johnny, how ya doin?"
"Fuck off."
"Hey Johnny, how bout that dime you owe me?"
"Fuck off."
You get the idea.

Johnny Fuck Off has a choice to make. He isn't much for choices. He always makes the wrong ones.
The choice to get high.
The choice to tell his boss to fuck off.

The choice to rob that goddamn Fiesta Mart with poor Jess sitting in the car.

The choice to run.

All bad choices. Choices that sent him to jail. Choices that got Jess killed. Sometimes he thinks he makes bad decisions on purpose. Bad decisions have a way of simplifying your life in a hurry. There aren't a lot of options out there for former meth-heads who just got out of prison. Find a place to live. Find a job. It was a simple plan but Johnny Fuck Off didn't care much for planning. He worked it all out in his head during the ride from Huntsville to Houston and was feeling pretty good about it until he stepped off the bus onto the scorching pavement. It was 105 degrees in the shade. Fuck Houston. And now he has another choice to make. The bus has let him off in front of a run-down apartment building called the Dolores Arms. It's two floors of chipped stucco and rusted security gates but the sign in the window offers efficiencies for $99 a week. Johnny suspects that Delores Arms caters mostly to crack whores and roaches but he's only got $11 dollars in his pocket and an uncashed check from the state for $172.18. His gut tells him to go inside and rent a room but Johnny is already starting to sweat and the Delores Arms sits across the street from an exotic dance club called Ooh La La. Johnny Fuck Off is thirsty. It's been a long time since he's tasted beer. Even longer since he's felt the touch of a woman's hand. In the end, it isn't such a hard choice to make.

*   *   *   *

5 dances
2 specials
1 hand-job
1 main stage
$623

Merry likes to make lists. She has kept a notebook of all her transactions for every club she has worked in—Treasure Hands, The Booby Hatch, and Pumps. One day, when she's too old to dance, she'll add them all up.

Merry closes the notebook and slips it inside her bag. All in all, she is having a pretty good day. Normally, Ooh La La is dead in the afternoon but today is the Friday before the 4th of July, and the club teems with men who knocked off early for the holiday weekend. They've been throwing a lot of money around too; anxious to get in an hour or two of tits and whiskey before they go home to wives that won't fuck them and girlfriends who stopped giving head, and the tv sets and barbecues and screaming children and firecrackers. Merry should clear around $300 after she tips out the DJ, waitresses, coat-check girl, house mom, and creepy Earl, who holds her hand as she steps on and off the stage. Then there's the cashier. She hates tipping the cashier. Why should she get tipped just for counting Merry's money at the end of the night?

She squeezes out a handful of lotion and begins to rub it all over her body. Merry does this at every break—a ritual that keeps her skin soft but also masks the odor of cigarettes and whiskey and unwashed hair and garlic sweat, and of the countless probing fingers that always smell faintly of semen and piss.

Merry wishes her efficiency had a tub, instead of that crappy little shower stall. Her feet hurt and it would be nice to soak them in a hot bath. If she can get in one more special this afternoon, maybe she'll take the night off.

*   *   *   *

It only takes Johnny ten minutes to blow through the 11 dollars in cash he had in his pocket when he walked into Ooh La La. The lunch time special is dollar Dixies but he only buys one beer. He spends the rest on the stripper with long chestnut hair. Johnny notices her right away. She has a face that makes him think of California and girls with skin that taste like salt water taffy. She has a face that reminds him of Jess.

Johnny takes a seat at the foot of the stage, watching intently as she slowly drops into a split before him. She's short but has long legs for her size.

"Aren't you all handsome!" she says with smile.

Johnny blushes. He knows she's just working him but there's a warmth to her voice that makes him want to believe she really means it.

"What's your name?" he asks.

"Meredith. But you can call me Merry."

She lifts herself up from the floor and moves closer to him. Johnny likes that she's not all inked up like the other girls. Her skin is unmarked, except for the tiny tattoo of a broken heart that sits between the thumb and forefinger of her right hand. He leans forward and presses a ten dollar bill into her fingers.

"I ain't seen anything beautiful in a long time."

Johnny gets up from his seat and heads to the bar. He wonders if they'll cash a check.

*   *   *   *

Arlee caught a vibe from Johnny the minute he walked into Ooh La La.

It was a familiar vibe, one he didn't like.

He didn't like the way Johnny tried to make small talk with him at the bar. There was an anxious formality to his speech that Arlee has learned to associate with ex-cons and delinquent, drugged-out army brats. It lurks beneath the surface of every "Yes, sir" or "Thank you, mam" uttered all too quickly by guys like Johnny—guys who corral their arms around bottles of beer and stacks of dollar bills as if they were the last taste of freedom they'd ever have. It nags at Arlee, like a lingering cold or an unanswered insult. He doesn't have anything against ex-cons. He figures if they did their time, then they deserve a shot at making things right, a chance to start over. He just doesn't want it happening here, not in his bar. In Arlee's experience, the Ooh La La isn't a place to start something new. It's a place to hide from the same old thing.

He has been avoiding eye contact with Johnny since he approached the bar. He walks the boards instead, emptying ashtrays and re-filling mugs of beer. Johnny tails him down the length of the bar.

"Hey, brother, can I get another Dixie?" he asks, with a hint of impatience.

Arlee frowns as he opens a longneck and pushes it

across the bar.

"One dollar."

Johnny pulls the check from his pocket and hands it to Arlee.

"Can you do me a solid and cash this, sir?"

He watches as Arlee eyes the check warily, silently mouthing the words, "State of Texas, Department of Corrections. "

Johnny knows it wouldn't be the first time Arlee cashed a check.

"This ain't no fucking bank. There's a Piggly Wiggly down the street that might do it for you."

Arlee drops the check on the bar. Johnny eyes him coolly as stands a little taller in his boots.

"Maybe I can cash that for you?"

Johnny turns to see Merry standing beside him. He smiles at her gratefully.

She takes the check from his hand and reads the amount. Without a beat, she pulls a wad of bills from her purse.

"Lucky for you I've had a good day."

She grins as she starts to count out the money. Arlee snatches the check from her hand.

"Get back on the stage, bitch. This doesn't concern you."

Johnny grabs Arlee by the wrist.

"You shouldn't talk to her that way. Say you're sorry."

Arlee wrenches his arm free and reaches for the length of rebar he keeps by the register.

"You're done, shit-bag. Get the fuck out of my club."

In one fluid motion, Johnny smashes his bottle of

Dixie against the bar and jabs the ragged neck into Arlee's stomach. He yanks the rebar from Arlee's fist, as the bartender collapses to the floor. He hears footsteps behind him and turns to see Earl closing fast. Johnny sidesteps him and strikes Earl across the head with the length of rebar. Earl goes down instantly, landing face-down on the floor. Johnny hits him several more times, the steel rod shattering Earl's skull. He doesn't look up until Earl has stopped moving. When he does, Merry is staring at him. She looks stunned. One of the girls is screaming and several customers are running for the door. Johnny extends a hand to Merry.

"We should get out of here."

*　　*　　*　　*

It never ceased to amaze Merry how violence just lied in wait, hidden among the weeds, like cats on doves. She had grown up with violence, seeing its mark left on her mother's face. There had been so many men since her daddy went away, uncles and stepfathers, and old business acquaintances. A few of them took an interest in Merry. Her mother would stand empty beer bottles next to Merry's door at night, so she would always wake if anyone tried to visit her while she slept.

Merry knew it would be wrong to go with a guy like Johnny, who clearly had anger issues. Still, she thought she should at least give him a ride away from Ooh La La. After all, he was only trying to defend her honor and up until the time he stabbed Arlee in the gut, had seemed kind of sweet. And then there were those hands.

She liked his hands.

Johnny and Merry pour out of Ooh La La, as patrons scramble for their cars.

Nobody wants to be near this scene.

Johnny's having second thoughts about gutting that bartender. Maybe he overreacted. In Huntsville, he learned to hit first and hit twice as hard as necessary. It was the only way anyone would give you any respect. But Johnny's not in Huntsville anymore. He's standing in a parking lot in Houston, only a few hours out of jail and already having killed a man. And now he's staring at the most beautiful girl he's ever seen and who's probably wondering if she's next on his list.

Merry leads Johnny to her car—a lime green Gremlin bestowed to her by her favorite aunt. Johnny stares at the old wreck, looking a little queasy.

"Not much of a getaway car, I know," quips Merry.

No response.

"You getting in or not?"

Johnny looks up at her, suddenly looking a little panicked.

"I don't know where to go."

It hits her then, that as crazed and volatile as he seemed inside Ooh La La, he was equally as lost now. A sad little puppy with blood on his shirt.

"You're not much of a planner, are you?"

He misses the joke.

"Just get in," she says.

Johnny sits down in the passenger seat, still looking a little dazed.

Merry reaches over and buckles his seat belt.

"What is it about strippers and strays?" she wonders.

NOBODY FUCKS IN CARS ANYMORE

From hotel room windows
I see only concrete and steel.
Each level of the parking lot reads
like a band of an ancient tree,
home to countless infidelities
and whispered confessions
carved into leather seats.

When we were teenagers we hitchhiked,
trading blowjobs for drug money,
stealing beer and cigarettes
from so many pick-up trucks.

Somehow the road felt less dangerous then,
though some of us were lost
to the music and highwaymen,
while others just forgotten
in the backseats of cars
mad with lip gloss and fingers
that smelled faintly of gasoline.

Better to hum with the pitchforks and engines
than sit idle in parked cars
alone and dreaming of a life
rich with oil and adventure.

WHAT FINGERS ARE FOR

these hands are too clumsy
to pick you flowers
and too dirty
to braid your hair

but they will clutch your throat
as easily as
my hand holds this pen

and these greedy fingers
will soil your lips
filling the spaces
where desire once hid

EVERYDAY CASANOVA

He fell in love at least once a day with the downy wisps of blond hair on the forearms of supermarket check-out girls; the strong freckled calves of postal workers; and the way that waitress at the diner would tie back her hair. And his heart swelled before the crude smile of the bartender, her mouth filthy with innuendo and the tired, glitter-stained eyes of the pole-dancer. He knew such love was transient; as fleeting as the laughter of drunks and dew on a blade of grass. It's such a shame when love turns to vapor and only the lovers remain.

WINDOW WATER ZOMBIES FUCKING

He lays on the bed, staring out the window at a tugboat in the harbor. It pilots a barge full of trash up the East River. He likes to watch the ships at work. He imagines the captains in their wheelhouses, leathery faces and nicotine-stained mustaches, drinking steaming cups of coffee in the salt air. She sits beside him on the bed, stretching.

"What are you looking at?"

"Harbor porn."

She grunts in acknowledgment as she arches her back and leans back on her elbows. The swell of her tits and long legs make him think of waves crashing on the beach. He wonders what she sees in him, his own body—scarred and tattooed—seems more akin to an abandoned factory, ancient and decaying. He could drown in her soft, tan skin.

She had spent the morning practicing yoga positions and telling him about a National Geographic Special she had watched on zombie ants. Deep in the forests of Brazil, a fungus invades the brain of an ant, compelling it to climb to the top of a tree, where the temperature and humidity provide the optimal environment for the fungus to sprout blooms from the ant's head. The story excited her and she fed it to him in breathless bits and pieces, as she moved from Downward-Facing Dog to

Locust and Peacock. He watched her movements, so graceful and controlled, as the morning sun found the small of her back, which grew damp with sweat while she described the blossoms emerging from an insect corpse. It was the most beautiful thing he had ever seen.

She is silent now. Her body calm as she slowly stretches out on the bed beside him. Her long yellow hair grazes against his chest, stirring a nipple to attention. He kisses her shoulder, still salty with perspiration, before burying his face between her breasts, breathing her in like the captain's first breath at sea. She plays with his cock, drawing him closer. He slips a finger inside her as she coils her body around him. It doesn't take long before they are fucking, her long legs raised up against his shoulders. They both watch as he slides his cock in and out of her pussy, his hands wrapped tightly around her thighs as she tickles his neck with her feet. He has grown to love her feet. He kisses them softly as they fuck.

He loses himself then, among the zombie ants and salt air and her toes against his cheek. And when he comes it is as if a flower has exploded from his brain. He no longer exists, except to feed the blossom.

ACCIDENTAL BETSY

I met her at a fuck party on the lower east side. She sat naked on the couch, reading a dog-eared copy of Tropic of Cancer. A raven-haired girl knelt before her, lapping at her cunt. An older man sat beside the naked girl, uncomfortably close—even for an orgy. He was wearing a grey suit. He watched them intently as he stroked his cock through his pants. I took a seat on the opposite side of naked girl.

"Now we're symmetrical," I said.

She looked up from her book and smiled. She reached out for my beer and took a long greedy pull before handing it back to me.

"I'm Betsy," she said.

She grabbed a fistful of the raven's hair and repositioned her head slightly.

"How can you concentrate well enough to read?" I asked.

"I can't," she whispered. "It's just a prop."

"Bringing Henry Miller to a sex party? A bit overkill, no?"

She laughed.

"I know. It's redundant but it was a special request."

"Do you mind?" said the older man, angrily. "You're fucking with my scene."

He flared his nostrils at me, like an old gray bull. A

tiny nugget of cocaine, hung from a hair in his nose. Betsy winked at me and smiled.

"Let's talk later."

Betsy and I left the party together at 4:30 am. We had coffee and hotdogs at Katz's Deli, holding hands beneath the table as we got lost in conversation. Her mind worked like some glorious pinball machine, bouncing from topic to topic, lighting up on long-forgotten tangents and shrieking with excitement. I fell in love with the lilt and meter of her voice, and her enthusiasm for the most obscure of details. It was morning by the time I walked her home to her studio on Ludlow Street. She pulled me into the doorway and kissed me softly on lips.

"Come upstairs with me," she said.

The floor of her apartment was covered with dirty laundry, old paperbacks, and pages ripped from magazines. A futon mattress sat on the floor in the corner of the room. Several canvases leaned against the wall, in varying degrees of completion. She used the walls of her apartment as her pallet. They were covered in steaks of color and dried-up globs of paint.

"Everything's a work in progress," she said with a laugh as she nonchalantly stripped off her clothes. She held out her hand to me.

"C'mon, let's fuck."

By the light of day, Betsy looked different than she had at the orgy. No longer disinterested, her body screamed of sex—a soft and creamy landscape drawn from spit and come. I spent hours exploring her body, languishing over every scar and bruise.

"I fall down a lot," she said self-consciously.

She sucked my cock, as she took swigs of orange soda and told me stories of her childhood in Indiana. We fucked for hours, pausing for the occasional cigarette or to let the air dry the sweat from our skin.

When I woke up, she was gone. She had left a note for me on her pillow.

Had to go to work. Call me some time.
-B.

I never got her number. I never saw Betsy again but sometimes I wake up at night with her voice in my ears and the taste of orange soda on my lips.

ANGEL'S SHARE

I look for you in the unlikeliest of places,
in smeared ashes on motel sheets
and the well-intentioned lies of hookers.

I catch glimpses of you in the seams of dark stockings
and the unbuttoned blouses of airport terminals,
hiding beneath fluorescent light and layers of civility.

I sense your sorrow in the sad-eyed woman who sits
alone
at the bus stop, the diner, and hotel bar,
and in the dull-smile that comes with a hand job.

I smell you in the hot breath of empty glasses and
cigarettes,
and in the musky, glittered fingers of the lap-dance girl,
painting my cheek in disappointment.
Again.

But I also smell you in the downy, leaf-scented hair
of coat-check girls, who have underwear that always
matches
and the audacity to dream.

And I hear you in the laughter of children
and the optimism of the drunk
and in the growls of hungry, feral cats.

So, I guess I'll keep looking for a little while longer.

THE NIGHT HOTEL (OR IT WAS SO NICE TO RECEIVE YOUR LETTER)

My night hotel grows weary,
vacant room by vacant room
teetering on its foundation
like those junkies on the corner
and drunks on rye
so precariously balanced on stools.

My night hotel grows weary,
fatigued by a savage cunt
that seduces me across
years of desert and neon lights
with such cruelty
that I pray for her death, not mine.

My night hotel grows weary,
drowning in the downy skin
and sweat-stained sheets
of tropical whores with names
that roll like Elysian Fields
and who carry your scent on my fingers.

WORDS ARE TOO FRAIL (OR FUCK ME UNTIL I DON'T FEEL SAD ANYMORE)

Words are too frail for my dirty work.
Language may be a virus
but there are other contagions
In my arsenal—
a plague of hot breath
spreading over your hips,
the pandemic of fingers
bruising breasts and thigh,
and an acid tongue
persistent as the rain
flooding your basement,
eroding the remnants
of those that passed before me.

CASUAL ENCOUNTER

They found him naked in the closet, a small puddle of semen at his feet. The necktie she had picked out for him at Barney's was drawn tightly around his neck. It was an anniversary gift. The police ruled it a case of auto-asphyxiation, even though there was evidence suggesting that he had not been alone in the motel room.

At first, the room terrified her. It was an old map, constructed of cracked wallpaper and towels that smelled of cigarettes and sweat, with no purpose other than to chart the trajectory of her husband's death. She would sit in the corner, staring at the closet doors, imagining remnants of him scattered throughout the room—the impression of his ass left on the mattress as he sat down to remove his shoes; his scent on the hand towels, which to her had always smelled vaguely of almonds; and the oil from his fingertips found on drawer handles and the remote control.

When she finally worked up the nerve to open the closet doors, she was surprised at how ordinary it was. You would never guess that someone had died in there. Her eyes scoured the carpet for semen stains but she could find no trace of him there. And while pieces of him seemed to haunt the motel room, the closet was completely devoid of his presence—notable only for its ordinariness. She wondered if that was why he had come to the motel, to escape the ordinary. How many people had he fucked here? She would never know.

She began to visit the room regularly. She liked to lie naked on the bed; the soft sheets cool to her skin. On sunny days, she would sit by the window and read a book. Over time, the room became hers. It was her dress folded over the chair; her lipstick on a drinking glass.

In the months that followed, she began to invite men to the room. They were never men that she knew. It was a simple matter to arrange; an ad on Craig's List that detailed her conditions. They were not permitted to touch her but she would watch them masturbate. If the mood struck her, she would undress for them. Sometimes, after a man had left, she would lie on the bed and touch herself; remembering the way he looked at her and the accelerated pace of his breathing as she stepped out of her dress. Desire could fill a room so quickly.

*　　*　　*　　*

Not knowing what else to do, he sat on the edge of the bed rubbing his cock through his pants. She was in a chair in the corner of the room, eyeing him coolly as she smoked a cigarette. She had barely spoken a word since he arrived. Her silence was relentless. It made him uneasy.

"So, how does this work?"

"Just like the ad said. You masturbate. I watch."

"Should I get undressed?"

"Whatever makes you comfortable."

He frowned. He had hoped their encounter would feel warmer, more intimate somehow. He at least thought she could show a little more enthusiasm. While he knew he had no reason to expect this, he could not help but feel a little disappointed.

He stood up and removed his tie. She watched him intently as he unbuttoned his shirt, her dark green eyes offering him nothing but the reflection of a burning cigarette. Still, it excited him to feel her eyes wash over him and his cock strained against his briefs as he stepped out of his pants. It was then that she shifted in her chair and he thought he detected a nearly imperceptible opening of her thighs. He wondered if he pleased her. He hadn't anticipated he would want to.

"Do you take off your clothes too?"

"Sometimes. If I feel like it."

He tried to imagine what she would look like naked—the curve of her hips, the color of her nipples. He wondered if she shaved her pussy. She sighed impatiently as she stubbed out her cigarette in the ashtray.

"Aren't you going to take those off?"

He removed his briefs. She stared at his cock, which had become fully erect. He could feel his face redden as a sly smile came to her lips.

"Do you do this often?"

She shrugged, showing annoyance.

"You ask a lot of questions. I just want to watch you jerk off."

He sat down on the bed and began to masturbate, parting his legs so she could see him more fully. Her breathing accelerated as she watched him. He closed his eyes and pictured himself kneeling before her, his lips pressed against her cunt. He imagined her hot breath filling the room like smoke.

"What are you thinking about?"

He opened his eyes to find her standing in front of him. Her sudden proximity was overwhelming.

"I was dreaming about your pussy; trying to imagine what it looks like."

"Would you like me to show you?"

The words made his bones ache.

"Please."

She unzipped her skirt and let it fall to the floor. She lifted her blouse up over her waist, so he could see her panties; simple pink cotton briefs. He could see the outline of her labia through the fabric. He began to stroke his cock faster.

"Does that excite you?"

He moaned.

"Come closer, then."

Instinctively, he reached for her. She recoiled and looked at him sternly.

"You're not allowed to touch me."

He nodded, indicating his understanding.

She stepped forward to the foot of the bed. Very slowly, he leaned closer until his mouth was nearly touching her thigh. She gasped. Her excitement was beginning to show through her panties. He breathed in deeply through his nose, taking in her scent. Her pussy smelled faintly sweet but earthy too. It reminded him of the woods after it rained. It made him feel feral. His cock throbbed in his hand.

"Please show me."

She slipped a hand inside her panties and slowly pulled them aside, revealing her vagina. He thought it was the most beautiful pussy he had ever seen, its flesh pink and glistening beneath a tiny patch of pubic hair as dark and mysterious as her eyes.

He came at once.

She picked up her skirt and went into the bathroom. She tossed him a towel before returning to her chair and lighting a cigarette.

"You should go now."

LET ME FIND POETRY

Let me find poetry
on the scraps of paper
that fall from your pocket
and in the patter of your feet
as you pace from room to room,
or in the cadence of your voice
reading words carved in the skin
of sailors of starts and sea.

Let me find poetry
in the warmth of your thighs
covered in spit and devotion,
or in the oasis of sweat
that pools between your breasts
under rough hands and bared teeth.
Poetry is never written,
it is only discovered.

I CAN ONLY OFFER YOU MY FLASK

I can only offer you my flask
and whisky lips that taste of want.
Let them find us panting
in bus stations
and dirty stairwells
with tongues that drip an ancient honey
and the moisture that pools in the small of your back.

I can only offer you my hand
and greedy tentacles that will part your thighs.
Let them find us gasping
in bathroom stalls
and commuter trains
our fingers glistening with spit and come
with eyes that see only dark corners and opportunity.

I can only offer you my mouth
and whispers that kiss your neck like rain.
Let them find us laughing
in soapy bathtubs
and tangled motel sheets
reciting bedtime stories with lips that smell of sex
familiar as the toothbrush shared by lovers.

I can only offer you my heart
and the secrets recorded on my skin.
Let them find us holding hands
on barstools
and in crowded airports
celebrating a life composed of stolen moments
because that is where love is born.

www.ingramcontent.com/pod-product-compliance
Lightning Source LLC
Chambersburg PA
CBHW030534130626
46552CB00006B/2253